SURRENDER

Part 2
Affairs of the Heart Series ~ Hollywood

KEW TOWNSEND

Tremmelle Publishing

HOLLYWOOD, CALIFORNIA

© 2016 Tremmelle Publishing. United States
© 2015 Cover Design by Sparkle Graphics
© 2015 Cover Layout by Jesse Kimmel-Freeman
© 2015 Cover images by Francis Gonzales; Jochen Schoenfeld
© 2014 Book Cover and Layout by BookDesignTemplates.com

Sign up for NEWSLETTER at www.kewtownsend.com

SURRENDER/ KEW Townsend
ISBN 978-06926440-4-1

Affairs of the Heart Series
Hollywood

BLOOD (Part 1)
LIASION (Part 3)
DECEPTION (Part 4)

Affairs of the Heart Series
London

HEART (Part 1)
TEMPTATION (Part 2)
PROMISES (Part 3)
DEVOTED (Part 4)
BETRAYAL (Part 5)

Sign up for NEWSLETTER

kewtownsend.com

CONTENTS

Chapter One

WANTED DEAD OR ALIVE

olly Hill stretched out each muscle beneath the pile of toasty comforters. A satisfied smile crossed her face as she reviewed her schedule for that day. Refreshed and eager she was ready for her new job, meet her new challenges and welcomed the first week of meetings at Cable Music Television (CMT).

Perched at the top of her list, to start researching the first guest on her show, *The Heart of Holly Would.* Astounded by Luka Hunter's wide range of connections he'd arranged for the long-awaited return of Marc LeRouge, the rock star cowboy.

Holly attempted to ignore the obvious, stubbornly aware of the ominous shadow of Kaine Walker, lead singer for *Hurrikaine*. He dawned in her memories as if to peek over her shoulder, flanking her around each corner. She would see him in less than thirty days at the wedding of his best friend Ian, the band's keyboard player, to the beautiful Solange, and that meant countdown mode.

To divert her rising obsession with Kaine's imminent

arrival, Holly took the hands-on approach, immersing herself in the details of her show. She worked endlessly with the set designers to get it right. She browsed many fashionable, antique clothing boutiques, searching for the right costumes to wear.

She'd lured her former legal assistant Lucy away from the old law firm. She laughed at how easy it was to convince her to work at CMT and rub elbows with the crème of the crop of the rock world.

Lucy left that day and joined Holly as her personal assistant. Holly was grateful because she was the best research assistant anywhere. Lucy's dark hair touched her shoulders and wore the fashionable loose maxi dress on her tall, lithe frame that looked out of place at the firm but fit in perfectly at CMT.

Yes, they'd found their niche in the world. Holly brought Lucy up to date on every facet of her romance with Kaine and the ever-attentive Luka Hunter.

Like everyone else, Lucy said she could never have made a choice. Yes, sweet Lucy, the only woman in her life she trusted. And yes, secrets continued to loom between her and Luka.

Lucy brought her bright, sunny, cheerleader smile with her this morning as she bounced in with an arm full of cassette and video tapes to add to the stack of magazines. Holly mulled over the concert footage, and it took longer to glance over the recent articles on Marc LeRouge's career. She looked for the hook, the angle no one probed. What would be her trademark, to make her show different from the glut of talk shows overloading the airwaves?

Lucy looked up and pointed out, "I like this research better than running down every sicko's lead on the Collins murder case."

Yes, Holly agreed. Everything seemed better free of the firm. All the long hours of research on the Collins murder trial caused Holly to grow closer to Lucy, and she loved her as a younger sister.

Impressed with Lucy's gift of ferreting through piles of printed matter to find the only angle not exploited, pleased Holly. Because of Lucy's talent, Holly gave her confidant the secret assignment, with strict instructions for Luka never to find out. Lucy would uncover any information she could unearth on *Hurrikaine* — the focus on Briarwood. She'd find out about that damn ghost or die finding out!

Holly spent hours on end with Lucy, sifting and selecting questions for her distinguished first guest. Late the next night Holly leaned onto her desk and confessed to Lucy.

"I like the process of learning about Marc in the same intimate way most fans connect with him. First, they love to listen to the music, and then read print matter, and lastly, watch the vivid video images portrayed of him. It must be hard for music fans to love their idols and never know them, at least not the flesh and blood of them."

And her hook for the first show arrived. And her observation caused her a moment's sorrow for Kaine, how isolated, yet familiar in households around the world, but no one knew the real Kaine Walker.

That was the way he wanted it, and she understood his need for her to love him for the real him. There wasn't any privacy for the rich and famous. Yes, Holly would ask Marc, he certainly would have a few choice answers on the subject, especially the isolation and exposure of fame.

Of course, Lucy did a meticulous job of briefing Holly on her findings. Holly wanted to be in on every facet of the production of the show. And Luka's constant enthusiasm encouraged her.

Luka as always, gave her the time she needed, his valuable suggestions, and spent long hours prepping her. Of course, Lucy fell hopelessly in love with Luka. The starved cat look moved on to her, and she followed him everywhere he went. But not enough to make the situation uncomfortable, she'd kept a respectful distance between them. Women following Luka was something Holly had to get used to, fast. A man like Luka bewitched every female that encountered him.

That night over dinner in Beverly Hills, Luka looked particularly handsome and acting very, very charming inquired casually.

""Cold Without You," that's your song?"

"Yes," she answered, wondering where he would go with this.

She added nonchalantly, "Could be Kaine thinking of me?"

"That's not what I asked. I asked if "Cold Without You" is *your* song. Did you write it?"

She swallowed quickly and proceeded as if trying to calm a provoked rattlesnake.

"Yes, I wrote it in London, early one morning. I inadvertently left it behind in Kaine's suite when everything unraveled. Why? Why would you ask me?"

"Because Kaine authorized you to receive credit as the sole songwriter which he bloody well should have since it's your piece."

"That's thoughtful?" She responded with the sting of a self-satisfied grin on her face.

"No, not thoughtful! The proper thing to do, it's your song. You will make quite a bit of money on this project. This song will become multi-platinum around the world. Do you play guitar as well as write songs?"

"I wouldn't call it playing. I can accompany myself if needed."

"Babe, you're too modest. I spoke with the session engineer Mo, in London this morning. He confirmed you played on the "My Lady" session. You will have a credit on the record sleeve as playing acoustic guitar on that song as well. Money seems to be attracted to you everywhere you go." He confirmed as his blue eyes sparkled.

Ever the executive she thought.

Holly replied, "It's not something that I'm used to doing. At the firm I made a decent living, Brett saw to that. But I worked hard for it. This is exciting, pure pleasure."

"And you'll continue to make more money than you can imagine. *Hurrikaine* is a machine, and its only purpose is to generate money. Everything it touches becomes gold."

Holly swallowed another gulp of her herbal tea. The rock world's increasing pace was moving faster.

Luka wore that expression on his face, ready to drop another of his famous bombs.

"Look, Babe, we have an opportunity here to do something entirely different with this show. I thought that at the end of each segment you and the guest would play guitars. The format is different, you, an accomplished woman, playing with the world's greatest male rockers. Though more women than ever are making it in rock music, it wouldn't hurt to bring a bit more equilibrium in a male-dominated rock music world. It might break new ground and a way for women to even the score. Who knows? If you sing, I'll record you. The sky is not the limit Babe, the sky is not the limit."

Damn.

Holly rubbed her cool fingertips over her forehead. She didn't want to be a damn pioneer. She wanted to do something she loved, woman or not. And especially, not to turn her show into a political statement. She didn't need to be the token 'politically correct' female at CMT.

She looked up reaching for her glass of tea.

"I would have never taken you for an advocate of women's liberation."

"Oh, I love women. They have all the power. Look at me. I'm helpless when I'm with you."

"Oh, I doubt helpless is the word I would use to describe you, Luka. You're anything but helpless."

He smiled his sunny Luka smile. But he'd made his point. With him, the sky was not the limit. That idea frightened her. She quickly jumped to a mental picture of her and Marc playing guitars together. She didn't know whether to laugh or cry. The thought sent a chill of another stab of fear through her. Facing a Grand Jury couldn't have brought out more fear in her. But her father's words flowed back in time.

You have the gift of adventure.

Follow it and never stop trying new things.

She managed to say. "You have a plan?"

"Well, I haven't worked out every detail. I needed to anticipate your possible reactions. But counting on a favorable one, I've lined up a guitar teacher to help you polish up each week and work with you on the selected closing song. Babe, we have something different with *Heart of Holly Would.*"

Luka was right. HHW might become exceedingly popular. And her enthusiasm began to equal his. Their eyes met. Luka held her gaze deliberately as if about to slip the hardness of him into her, exactly like what she thought making love with him would be. The challenge of the deal, it excited Luka.

Holly finally understood what made her different from other women. She'd been the one Luka made love with all day and all night. She'd discovered a way to make love with Luka, through his work because his work was him.

Holly planned to know everything about Luka, at least as much as he'd allow.

She trusted Luka Hunter more each day. He hadn't mentioned the CMT acquisition yet to her, but confident he would soon.

They sat out of breath, the excitement of the project coursing in their veins, staring at each other as if they'd been making hard, nasty love. And they both recognized the show would become a success.

Holly broke the spell first.

"It will work Luka but only if you help me and stay near me, but to play with Marc LeRouge?"

And Holly glanced to the window. "I'm looking forward to seeing Marc again. I remember his kindness to me at Friar Manor. And since we shared an incriminating photo in all the London rags, it will give me an opportunity to apologize for the unflattering coverage he received because of me. I had no idea I would become sensational news overnight."

"I did! If I have anything to do with it, Miss Hill, you will be a household name before the year is finished."

Holly spent the rest of the evening with the writers of *Heart of Holly Would*, constructing interview questions, getting each aspect the way she wanted.

Later at a restaurant catering to the after hour clientele, she remarked to Luka.

"It's incredible how many hours are wrapped up in preparation for a little twenty-two-minute show."

Luka agreed and smiled warmly, "It won't be a little show for long, Babe. Hold on to your bleedin' hat, you're about to crash the party." His blue eyes sparkled while he took her hand in his.

Yes, Luka knew it all!

Finally, the big day arrived and found Holly's nerves brittle but confident, as a result of being over-rehearsed, on both the guitar and dialog. She sat twisting her script into a telescope, listening to the camera and lighting man map out their course of action. As if a stone was thrown into a quiet pond, she sensed in her psyche, a strong magnetic presence ebbing all about her.

Holly turned her head, and her eyes followed a pair of old, black, leather cowboy boots heading her way. She naturally let her scrutiny trail up the legs, noticing trim, well-defined thighs, clad in fitted, lightly brushed, blue denim pants. Her eyes raised one notch at a time as she continued to scan this magnetic presence.

Her gaze was settled on the waist length, lustrous, black, leather jacket and peeked inside to find a crisp, white, shirt, with an open, banded collar. The rock cowboy, Marc LeRouge, had arrived.

Holly dared to lift her gaze to rest on Marc's handsome face. His sculptured good looks confirmed incredibly handsome and sexy Marc. How had she forgotten? Perhaps it had been too dark, or one too many glasses of champagne at Friar Manor? Or, too in love with Kaine to see beyond him?

Marc's face filled with a prominent note of recognition as Holly rested her eyes on his enchanting and intelligent blue eyes. She caught herself and her thoughts, hoping she hadn't made a colossal fool of herself. Nevertheless, Marc's magnetism unnerved her. Marcs' brawny, clean-shaven, lightly tanned face came close to Holly.

He politely extended his hand, saying enthusiastically.

"Holly, good to see you. How's London?"

"You remember London?"

"Who wouldn't? People were asking me for weeks about meeting Kaine's Mystery Woman. The photo of us in the *London Daily News* and the international tabloids helped a bit," he teased. Then he sent her a comforting smile. He seemed unaffected by her headlines since London.

"Yes, you're right, of course, all unfortunate timing, Marc. I'd like to apologize for any embarrassment I may have inadvertently caused you or your family by those awful photos."

"Unfortunate? Those photos were fine. I would say the unfortunate photos were the ones of you with Luka at the beach. I was in Europe when I saw them…"

Marc glanced away to let the sting of the embarrassment pass.

As she realized what his words meant, she gasped, taken aback, because she hadn't realized, her many guests saw her in the buff, nude, naked! Not to mention, along with any horny, or twisted fans in her audience that wanted to see her naked body. All they needed to do was track down a European rag.

She was at a disadvantage.

Marc smiled, glancing at her.

He purposely tried to keep his eyes from sweeping down her body, attempting to put her at ease. It didn't work. It made things quite clear how life would be from this point forward. She recognized what everyone would be seeing when they looked at her, right down to her birthday suit.

"It's okay." Marc consoled easily. "I'm used to the press. You will be after a while. It comes with the territory. I'm glad to see you've weathered the media storm this far."

What she wanted to scream to Marc, she hadn't weathered the raging storm. She wanted to explain how her fairy tale romance with Kaine fractured soon after their well-documented meeting and sent her into a deep, dark depression. She wanted to share many intimate feelings with this tall and friendly man, who stood before her, comfortable with himself and his fame.

She needed answers.

But, of course, she didn't ask.

She needed to remain a professional. But the ah-ha

moment arrived, and she found the focus of her questions to Marc. And she knew Marc would tell her.

Holly looked at him, noticing his pierced ears, filled with shimmering gold hoops and like Kaine, one stud accented his left ear. His once long, rocker, sun-streaked outlaw hair, clean-cut to his shoulders, with the sides of his windswept hair back. Short locks of feathered hair, covered his forehead framing his charming face.

Marc had definitely refined his raw outlaw image. And he didn't seem to care that every woman on staff at CMT clamored about to catch a glimpse of him.

Lucy's research revealed Marc matured to become a wealthy and successful businessman, with a long string of hits by the band and a meteoric solo career. His estimated worth meant Marc LeRouge never needed to work another day of his life. But somehow, these men needed connection only the stage would bring. Someday, she hoped she would understand how that worked. Especially, how it drove these men.

Holly had seen this specialized power in Sheridan, Wyoming, the last night of the clandestine meeting at Michael's when the socially reclusive multi-millionaires met secretly to make one more deal.

What was the connection between them that drew them? She allowed a wry smile, snapping herself out of her self-imposed trance. She handed Marc a copy of the interview questions she'd worked on for days and then added.

"Sorry, I won't be asking you any of these. Instead, get comfortable, kick-back and let's talk."

"Sounds like Presidential fireside chats, only its rock music," Marc pointed out with a grin curling about the edges of his lips.

Remember this intimate comfort zone.

Holly chanted the words maniacally as if magical to herself because Luka strived for this mood.

"Exactly the way I hoped you'll feel when we're finished. If you feel that way, then the audience will feel the same like they have been privy to a private chat."

Marc nodded in agreement.

Holly turned her head. Someone called for her to make another decision.

Marc turned out to be the perfect first guest, exactly as charming as at Friar Manor and more at ease than she'd been for hours. Yes, she'd had faith that she would succeed with the first taping without falling flat on her face.

As it neared showtime, Holly's wardrobe call arrived. She changed into her dark-blue, velvet pants and fawn-colored, gauze, blouse and then slipped into a brocade vest and waist-length, dark blue, velvet coat.

Her hairdresser painstakingly strived for a natural, wind-stirred effect while her make-up took half an hour to look natural. She attempted to appear casual and unaffected, not expecting an old friend to drop in unannounced, to catch up on the latest news in the music industry.

The set of HHW dark and atmospheric with a soft lighting, had a high-back brushed-velvet, avocado-green antique couch. Beside that a black, wicker table to complete the ambiance. The obligatory nineteen twenties Tiffany lamp had an intricately beaded shade. Dark, rich tapestries hung lush and flowing on the walls on each side of her. No one would have guessed the set extended, but a few feet on either side of the couch.

A simulated open window, between the curtains, looked out upon a setting like a Garden of Eden that resembled the scenery around her place in the canyon. Of course, a gentle breeze blew the lace curtains inward. The dark atmosphere oozed light, airy, and friendly, but most of all private and secluded, a safe place where secrets are revealed. She'd insisted on this mood.

Luka, wonderfully supportive of her vision, had coached her endlessly.

"You will be sitting on the couch, close enough to touch your guest. Break the rules, cross the invisible line, reach out, and become intimate. Make it natural, not contrived in any way or the camera will pick it up. Remember you can't fool a camera.

"This is a dialog between two close friends. Look for the intimate point-of-view. You're asking the questions meant only for a close confidant — that's the core of your show. Only you, Holly, would ask them. You will ask all the personal questions the press will never get a straight answer. The more controversial the topic matter, the deeper you plunge. This will never be the usual interview show. You will not chronologically list the guest achievements and showcase their current project — except on guitars.

"You'll highlight the hopes and fears of your guest. Feelings will stay with people while they are buying another CD or concert ticket.

"People buy tickets to see whom they know, like, and love. When you're finished, they'll know more about the guest. Their career blunders, the lonely lifestyle of performers, and any current elicit affairs of heart and money."

It seemed like Luka wanted the impossible from her.

Didn't he always?

Luka pressed her, challenged her, he'd taught her to follow his directions from the first moment he'd held her in Chelsea, directing her to walk with him. She would find a way to please him.

Didn't she always?

"You're the hook, Holly — not the guest! You're the natural. You're fresh from a terrible beating from the bloodied hands of the media. You're an innocent that's been violently raped by every conceivable form of media known to show business. Only you can bring a tender, experienced heart to your interviews. You bring the compassion never extended to you.

"I want you to pour out your infectious personality, to provoke laughter and then tenderness, to squeeze tears from your guest, the more personal, the more human, better for ratings. I'm confident you can do this without compromising the integrity of your guest."

After that pep talk, Holly reeled for days. She carried the impossible responsibility as her wobbly, stage-frightened legs supported her when she approached the stage platform. She bumped against the terracotta tea set, and the clinking sound brought her to her senses.

Time to step up to her obligations. This was her show. It was up to her to make sure she put out a product she was proud of because she'd finally realized her focus. Her strength — to sell intimate information. She sat knitting her fingers together, anticipating the next moment, the real beginning of her new life. And then Luka hollered the word that both excited and terrified her.

"Action."

Marc approached the set, impressive and self-assured. Why not? How many thousands of interviews had he'd done? She turned her face, acknowledging Marc simulated knock at the door. He entered with a big, warm smile gracing his handsome face. She exchanged an awkward hello, taken aback by his continued good looks. She leaned near him, ignoring every professor's lecture on the sterile art of interviewing at the law school. She impulsively crossed over the professional boundaries, reached out, and warmly hugged Marc.

Her show started.

After inviting him to get comfortable, Holly took off her jacket, threw it on the back of the couch to join him, and started to pour her guest tea. It seemed longer than the scheduled thirty minutes. She held pages of material to cover when the interview time ended because they'd taken too much time laughing.

She heard Luka say.

"Keep talking."

Obligingly, Holly leaned in and asked. "What have you been working on in the studio?"

Marc offered. "Here, let me play a bit."

And Holly followed the cue cards saying, "Yes, let's play."

Of course, Luka spent sufficient time building her self-confidence to make her realize she'd already played with the best musicians in their profession when she'd recorded "My Lady" in London with Kaine and Ian.

She leaned, picked up her beautiful Martin guitar, a gift from Kaine named Slick. It had been waiting for her off camera on a stand. Marc pulled an Ovation guitar from behind the couch and began to pick a sweet acoustic version of his latest single. Holly joined in on the opening bars and after a few minutes, the signal arrived to set down the guitars, but she and Marc played long after the cameras stopped.

Holly's head spun — her first show wrapped.

Frank, the editor, would have a taskmaster's job editing the best of their dialog. But her first show rested in the can. She couldn't restrain herself from lavishing Marc with high praise for his grace, charm, and insights.

"Thank you, you've made my job seem like a visit with a dear friend. You were wonderful, expressive, and exciting. Everyone will love your humorous road antidotes."

She paused and then added, "I can't thank you enough for today."

Holly lingered in the warmth of his radiant smile, only a second. With an impulsive motion, she unprofessionally reached out and hugged him again. Marc would leave a lasting imprint on her. He would always be special, her first. And wasn't it true? A woman never forgot her first.

"Thanks again Marc."

She realized no one warned her or explained that she might have strong feelings of attraction toward her influential guests. She wondered if it was possible to cross the intimate line into a guest's private, inner sanctuary, and not experience something for them emotionally.

Later Holly and Luka paced impatiently around the set, annoying the technician, waiting for the videotape to playback the show. Frank brought it up, and she sat holding Luka's hand.

Something happened, changed.

For the first time, Luka didn't stir her in the manner as Marc. What changed inside her? Had Luka become too predictable and comfortable?

CMT purposely shot more tape than needed. And the thrill of seeing her image on the screen amazed her. How well she'd camouflaged her raging anxiety.

And Luka, always her champion, boosted any sagging confidence with a watershed of compliments.

"You showed all your warmth and kindness, Babe. See how you put Marc at ease? Yet you allowed enough tension to carry it off, and the time you reached out and covered his hand with a compassionate gesture of friendship, a bloody masterpiece. Miss Hill, you have a hit!"

"You mean, *we*!" Her heart said Luka was right.

He continued the flowing praise and Holly lapped up every word.

"The show appears as if by accident the viewer has stumbled onto an intimate conversation between old friends, catching up on gossip and news, only they are the top musical phenomena of our time. The closing scene with the pair of you playing the opening chords to his new song, purely inspirational. Watch, it will set new industry standards for music, talk shows."

She'd never seen Luka that ecstatic.

"HHW is a refreshing change from the staid and common interview, which plagues the airwaves. Holly, hold on, in my professional opinion you're going to become a household name. If you think the press hounded you closely before, well, you can kiss what's left of your private life goodbye."

Holly dropped Luka's hand. The chill numbed her insides. Luka was right. She would indeed become big news. How frightening that Luka forgot that quickly.

Or, had he?

Was this a gentle nudge?

A wake-up call?

The time would come when she'd have to name the father. She needed a few more weeks to hold on to her privacy, to sort her life out.

For the time being, she would keep her secret from Kaine.

Chapter Two

LET IT GROW

Holly attended the Heart of Holly Would (HHW) pilot party down the corridor at CMT. Marc appeared and offered to call Holly when he returned to L.A., between April and May of his newly launched world tour. The news made her realize if Kaine missed the wedding, the American stadium dates would bring him here for sure.

Too many glasses of champagne later, everyone headed in different directions, Marc bid goodbye, to catch the red eye. Marc spread his charm around the room and then vanished.

Holly sank into the closest chair. She'd finished the last of her mineral water and longed for a long, hot soak in her tub when the next surprising invitation arrived.

Luka sauntered up real close to her, and she leaned back against him. His arms enclosed her in a gentle embrace. He boldly pressed his cheek to hers and whispered close to her ear.

"Why don't you come up to my bachelor pad?"

He'd spoken so quietly she almost didn't hear him. Luka certainly stirred her curiosity with the invitation. She postponed a soak in the tub for an evening with Luka.

She welcomed the cold caress of the evening as the crisp December breeze blew her hair. Luka drove a new car, a classic green Jaguar, probably a condition of the new deal as he drove along talking on his car phone.

This is his new office.

She looked over at the man that controlled CMT amazed at her good fortune.

Luka drove east on Sunset Blvd., heading to the Sunset Strip where he unexpectedly turned north up Sunset Plaza.

She thought of all the time he spent at her cottage in the canyon. She'd figured that after her visit to Malibu, he went to the beach whenever he left her. And when no time, lived in a cramped apartment or condominium because he'd never invited her. She sat ready to see what Luka called his "bachelor pad."

Luka climbed high to the top of the West Hollywood mountain. Then drove down a cutback road and up again along the side of a hillside, and around another narrow road that wrapped around the hill like the red stripe on a candy cane. Once he reached the top of the mountain, a large, thick fence spread its wings along both sides hiding the compound. He produced a card, and the gate opened, reminiscent of Kaine's entrance to Briarwood.

But this was not Briarwood.

Luka followed another long twisted driveway to a circular drive.

"Luka! This is your bachelor pad?" She exclaimed with the same amazement when she'd learned of the extravagant "boat," but bewildered as she gazed out upon the tremendous view of the bright, liquid lights twinkling below her feet. The entire Los Angeles basin spread out for his approval. He sat perched up there on his exclusive summit, with the San Fernando Valley behind them, L.A., on the other. Commanding luxury — that's how the man with the controlling stock in CMT lived.

The last count, he owned this magnificent mansion, the exquisite beach house in Malibu, and a gift, a 120-foot yacht. After all these months, she wondered who the hell Luka Hunter was.

Then came the haunting question.

Why in the hell did he want her? She didn't doubt herself just postulating a reality check.

Catching her breath, she scolded.

"This place is an astounding bachelor pad, Luka! Here in Hollywood, we call them mansions, if they called grand old buildings like this a mansion, any longer. A hotel would be more fitting. How many rooms?"

Luka smiled and laughed.

"I'm not certain. I don't usually like my living quarters this large. I prefer intimate, cozy settings. I'm told I need more investments besides the beach house and a place for important guests to hang out. I have more rooms than I need, counting the outside bungalows."

He smiled sheepishly and let a long lock of hair cover his face.

Luka gave Holly the ten-cent tour and apparently lost his interest in the grandeur of the monument to a lost time unimpressed with his grand lodging as he'd been with his boat. When they finished, she'd lost count of the bathrooms in the four-story mansion. In one wing, she'd found many bedrooms, a massive library, complete recording studio, a bowling alley, two formal dining rooms, a screening room and a beautifully spacious living room, with a picturesque window that exposed the same imposing view of the valley. Luka's living arrangements were hard to accept and left her astonished.

He asked, "Let me show you the pool?"

She followed him.

He briefly commented on a small cottage in the back once used as the servant's quarters but turned out to be three times the size of her family's home in Santa Barbara.

He saw her amazement and explained.

"The house, built in the late twenties, apparently a dream of a studio mogul."

As you are now, she thought.

"Part of the deal included the original furnishings."

He brought her back full circle to stare at the magnificent, winding wrought-iron staircase in the main entry. Holly was positive Norma Desmond would descend the staircase to ask Mr. DeMille for her stage directions. But no shaking of her head or opening and closing of her eyes was going to make this be a dream. This was where Luka Hunter called home.

She stopped and stared at him, recognizing she didn't have much of a clue who Luka was. He was remarkably complicated, and the things that power and money afforded him were astonishing. And yet, he seemed unaffected and comfortable being Luka Hunter. It was time to change Lucy's assignment, time to do an extensive background check into who the hell was Luka Hunter.

Luka stopped talking, and she didn't know how long he'd been silent.

"There I've become a bloody bore. I hate them. I'm sorry Babe, where are my manners. Would you like supper or something to drink?" He offered before sweeping her into his familiar embrace and tightened his arms around her perfectly after months of practice.

"I don't need anything but you, thanks anyway. I'm dumbfounded by your bachelor pad. I'm convinced this house has seen the A-list of Hollywood's various eras flow in and out of its secretive doors."

"Many secrets no doubt. And it will have our secrets to keep too." Luka's face flushed.

Could it be he was a bit embarrassed by his wealth? As an Englishman, he hated to flaunt the obvious. She'd learned that much being around him. What would he think if he knew she was aware he owned the controlling stock in CMT? It was then she realized that he certainly would be able to afford a house of this size and magnificence in any port he desired in the world.

What a thought!

Luka continued, "*Hurrikaine* has proved to be a predictably lucrative business venture for me. But if I am to confess, this property is not as large as my father's estate in England, but a start and paid for with cash."

"It's your fixer-upper?"

"What's that?"

"A feeble attempt at humor, never mind." But she hadn't missed his reference — not as big as my father's manor. Hadn't he once told her he lived near Kaine? And Sarah

Cromwell. Hadn't Luka told her Sarah's father worked as the groundskeeper next door to Kaine? These men had a funny way of looking at being neighbors. Between them, they must own the entire English countryside. And that explained why he's not impressed with these residences because to him they're not up to the standards of his childhood home.

Luka smiled, not understanding her fixer-upper joke, and added caught in a moment of confession.

"You mustn't forget the flat in London."

Holly laughed again and to tease him.

"I can well imagine what you'd call a flat in England. Does it rival the size of Briarwood?"

His facial expression didn't respond to her joking. It quickly grew hard, and his lips thinned while the sparkle drained from his eyes. He spoke with an edge of irritability in his voice.

"Well, not quite, but I'm telling you this for a reason, not to go on being the braggart. You understand why Tessa's interested in all my holdings. She wants the big money. We don't have the California divorce laws. She doesn't wish to split the properties with me."

He suddenly yawned breaking his solemn mood. He quickly dismissed his marital problems, slipped his arms behind her tighter, and pulled her closer.

"Let's have our private celebration out here since the pilot for HHW is in the can."

Luka released her, and she followed him farther out, to a lavish, well-manicured yard to rival any Hollywood back lot. It was massive. It came equipped with the obligatory indoor and outdoor sparkling swimming pool. The crystal-clear water reflected a kaleidoscope of colors from the backlit waterfall and landscape, reminding her again of a giant DeMille movie set. The midnight sky, clear and moonless, allowed her to fade into dreams of this style of lavish living as she stared out into the night.

Luka came close and turned her face to his, so close, too close. His arms moved to the place they always went, to brace the small of her back.

Holly leaned into his warm body.

He kissed the top of her head and spoke quietly, almost a whisper.

"From where I stand, I see L.A., as yours, and soon the country. Next year the show will go international, starting with CMT-UK, and then Europe, after that you'll have the world. The sky is not the limit Babe. I guided Kaine to the top giving him the world. Let me give you the moon."

"The moon?"

No wonder these kinds of men hid away. They kept their vast holdings a guarded secret. Luka was as afraid as Kaine. Of course, they shared the same fear of not being loved for themselves, but also sharing their vast wealth and worldly trappings.

And like a thunderbolt, was that it? Had Luka been cautiously testing her at every turn? It would seem she passed each hurdle with high marks, because she stood in his private sanctuary, wondering how many more secrets of Luka's she would need to keep to be awarded all access.

"You're going to be a big star, Babe. And you're going to need a personal manager, someone familiar with all the facets of the music business. Someone able to guide you in major career decisions. You know I can do that, Babe, and more. I can because I care what happens to you. Believe me. I'd do my best to look out for your interest."

The alarm sounded inside Holly. Luka was unbelievable. Were there no ends to his sacrifices to keep her involved in his life?

"I believe you, Angel Eyes. You've always looked out for my best interest since our first meeting in London. It's strange, how fate has worked things out isn't it?"

"What has fate to do with it?"

She didn't answer.

Luka didn't press for a response.

Holly leaned back in his arms, marveling at the power and manipulation it would have taken from him to have masterminded all the events. Seemingly, none of this surprised him.

"Luka Hunter. Who are you?"

But she hadn't realized she'd spoken the words aloud.

"You want to know who I am. Now, you ask. A few think I am the devil personified, others like you, have believed me to be their guardian angel. I'm neither good nor evil. I am a man Babe, a man with deep feelings and strong needs. I'm like you. I make mistakes, have hopes and dreams. I'm sorry to disappoint you, but I am simply flesh and blood."

It wasn't the response she'd imagined.

And then Luka kissed her lips lightly, full of restraint, and she wanted to cry out.

Let go Luka. Let go.

He didn't let go, and she looked at him, the always beautiful and sexy Luka, never far from his phone, a ridiculously wealthy man, intimidating and powerful. The more exposed to him she was, the more he began to scare her. And if Kaine rejected her at the wedding, she would most likely fall madly in love with him, or worse. It may have already happened, and she, nor Kaine, could do a damn thing to stop it.

She'd barely finished her analysis because it was as if he'd read her mind. Luka bent his head closer to hers. She had paused before she pressed her lips to his. She ran her tongue along the seam of his lips until he opened his mouth to allow the tip of her tongue to dip deep inside where she kissed him with great passion. All the while, he remained restrained.

To be with him was all she wanted.

His words — *sky's not the limit* — made her remember her future, a bright future with him.

As it was turning out — her only future.

Chapter Three

LOVE IS ON THE WAY

Time had been merciful. Holly logged three shows wrapped and in the can by mid-December and met two, more of the elite rock stars of the music world. Her emotional response cooled with each guest. No more powerful reaction like with Marc. Yet the music men were influential, magical, and talented. She loved spending all her time surrounded by the creative musicians. Her every thought of music and music men followed her into her meetings, rehearsals and, of course, the many hours of research.

Lucy turned up nothing new on Briarwood or Luka. Holly sat with Lucy until late into the night in the canyon, ferreting through long-forgotten angles on the rockers lives with a fine-toothed comb. Holly proved to be a gracious hostess on HHW, and as with the Collins murder trial, a damn good investigator. Holly couldn't afford any mistakes on the air and felt confident she'd unearthed every possible secret. Yet she'd found comfortable, new ways, of ferreting out the hidden answers from her famous and occasionally media-shy guests. The holiday season dictated she needed to attend a few local music benefits on Luka's arm that she'd become a rising television personality. And it seemed that Luka permeated every crack and corner of her life, except her bed.

Sometimes she would lapse back into old insecurities and figured Luka was playing her for a fool. He'd been looking for a woman to turn into a star for his first venture into television when he took over the helm of CMT. She was nothing more than a commodity. Other times, he seemed sincere and genuine and then she'd reek of guilt over her doubts about him. Luka Hunter was complicated and impossible to figure out.

Holly's always cautious father, when it came to signing a name to the paper, encouraged her to sign a six-month personal manager's contract with Luka to see if she enjoyed working with him. Though Luka charmed Arthur Hill and her mother, Anne, her father was a businessman first. He saw how much Luka loved his daughter and told Holly that. He'd given her his blessing, wholeheartedly, but business was business. And that was what Holly tried to explain to Luka, rationalizing it as her father had.

"I consider this limited action the best move I can make for myself. If we have a falling out, I wouldn't want us to be tied to each other by a long, drawn out contract."

Luka's face grimaced, and in his 'I always get what I want," tone of voice said, "We're not going to have a falling out, Babe."

Holly retorted. "Course you're right. But it's been known to happen, look at you and *Hurrikaine*. Plus, you and I share a unique relationship. Who knows where it will lead?"

Luka dismissed her argument about his being on the outs

with the *Hurrikaine* family, and Luka quick to answer.

"It will lead where you allow it."

And he kissed her once again, with his restrained passion, burning deep in his blue eyes so blue.

Day by day, Holly's baby grew larger with no satisfactory paternal arrangements made.

She received a memo from Michael announcing the next guest. Michael's memos usually meant he was about to change her life. She sat stationary at her desk reading the words, hoping for a mistake.

"No!" She protested.

Holly called Michael's office to check it wasn't a horrible joke. But it hadn't been. The excitement in his voice said, 'don't tell me no.' She listened to his shocking words.

"We've lined up Ian Montgomery, for an interview here at CMT."

That was fine, welcomed. But that wasn't the bomb.

"Then we're going to cut in with CMT-UK by satellite and have you interview Kaine live. I've been informed he has recovered from his virus, and he's willing to be interviewed. But, he'd demanded one stipulation. Understandably, he wants you and no one else to interview him. We'll deliver the global scoop on HHW, the reunion of Kaine with the Heart of the *Hurrikaine*."

Holly sat thunderstruck. The word *Kaine* reverberated in her soul. Where had the time flown? As Michael's words echoed in her head.

His virus — recovered.

Kaine's hospital stay escaped her since starting HHW. She'd occasionally heard the radio jockey announce how the media was looking for the reclusive Kaine Walker. She realized she'd been busy, and that, Emily hadn't contacted her in almost a month.

What happened?

Did she care?

Holly only knew she was not ready to face Kaine, not anytime soon, but for a different reason, she was growing close to Luka. Only Kaine could make her forget Luka as only Luka could make her forget Kaine. And that was her dilemma, wasn't it?

That afternoon Michael called an emergency meeting to discuss a never before use of satellite technology. CMT was about to embark on this Trans-Atlantic interview joining Kaine and Holly together as if they were in the same room.

Holly wondered what Luka knew? Had this been his brainchild? It was Luka's special talent to create sensational headlines for ratings.

Outside Michael's office, Luka unnerved her by asking bluntly.

"Have you heard from Solange?"

It was happening all over again. *Hurrikaine* was starting to lap at the edge of their relationship. The storm was on the horizon.

"Only a message from her for my final fitting of my bridesmaid's gown next week. It's been moved to the Asset boutique in Beverly Hills this time. But Solange has been elusive since the holidays started."

That was the first time she'd vocalized that she was part of the wedding party. He didn't flinch, but she knew Luka. He either already knew or was way ahead of her, understanding she would see Kaine again, and soon, or was planning his next move.

Where was everyone? Holly took a quick inventory of her life, there was no surprise. Her current world revolved around only one, Luka. Of course, the newspapers and tabloids reported on their social and professional comings and goings with great detail. One reporter from *Rock 'n' Roll World* flattered her, saying her show.

> *Holly Hill has ingratiated herself to the rock community as only a battered survivor of the press can. Miss Hill's guests seem to be willing to open up to her in a way unparalleled.*

Of course, there were opposing critics that complained that she slept with each guest and acquired the information through the osmosis of pillow talk. And all the tabloids swore they had the exclusive interview with a *close source* that knew for a fact she was sleeping with Luka. Someone reported she moved into his compound, the *Dream Catcher,* or the Dream as Luka had come to call it.

All were lies.

All untruths.

She'd come a long ways in three months to become a seasoned pro, and knew it was nothing to get excited about, in fact, it was nice for once, to read a few pleasant words about her. How had Kaine survived all the years of scrutiny?

There it was again.

That word.

Kaine.

How insidiously, the word started to slip into her everyday thoughts. He'd supposedly recovered from his virus. Translated, that meant Kaine was coming.

Kaine, in a little over two weeks.

She would interview him in days.

Holly thought back to the magazine reviewer's kind words. He'd given her a sense of arrival, validating her new confident feelings she'd gained with each show behind her.

But the continuing, pressing question — what to do with Kaine?

Kaine would be on a digital computer transmission, and she didn't pretend to understand the revolutionary new technology, but it meant she would finally talk to Kaine face-to-face.

Her thoughts consisted of the oddest scenario.

Would she scoop herself and tell him of their love child?

The child that bonded them together forever.

Of course, she wouldn't do that on international television, she argued with herself. But there were many questions. Would she be able to remain professional with Kaine? Once she saw his incredible blue eyes, would she be able to accept his scorn and rejection over the nude shots with Luka?

Oh, how this happened?

Her thoughts spiraled downward quickly, throwing her into a new depression she couldn't shake. Its power threatened to force her to hide in the canyon.

She turned her thoughts to this side of the Atlantic, looking forward to having Ian as a guest on her show. She must arrange to see him privately, noting she'd not seen him since he'd boarded the *Hurrikaine* Super Star jet in London, bound for Paris, the city where she should have married Kaine. How quickly things fell apart and changed those last few days in London, the city where she'd fallen in love, and her life should have started — instead was torn to shreds. And too much had happened these past few months to hope for Kaine's change of heart.

Dinner, that night at the Dream, had been simple take-out. Luka had taken up residence in a four thousand square foot guest suite in the corner of the compound, utilizing a small upgraded guest kitchen overstocked by his butler Pierce; she'd met on Luka's yacht the Day Dreamer.

The guest bedroom included a luxurious adjoining spa/bath. He rarely moved from these three rooms. In his mammoth bedroom, sat a plush leather couch, and home entertainment center, with the latest state-of-the-art surround sound. The wall-sized screen afforded them every advantage when scouting for new candidates to run on CMT.

The future of the established, as well as new bands, sat in Luka's talented and capable hands. Luka bore an awesome responsibility, one she wouldn't take on for any amount of money.

He must enjoy the power, but why did he need it?

Burrowed in his embrace, close enough to feel his heart beating, she announced.

"I find watching new and upcoming videos of talented bands invigorating. Especially, with the wave in music quickly changing these days. It seems as if last week's videos became the rising stars. What happened? One's dead, and the other one is missing in action. It's hard to predict the next rage in music or potential candidates for my show."

"Don't worry, your show will have a freshness to it other's don't have. Over time, you will come to understand the transformations and trends going on in the music world. Remember Babe, with me, the sky is not the limit."

"With you around to remind me, I'm starting to believe you more and more every day." She leaned into him as he pulled his arms around her tighter, more protectively. But her thoughts were deceiving and strayed to Kaine.

Holly wrestled with the same old thoughts.

Whether to tell Kaine about their child or not.

She snuggled up against Luka's royal blue, button down, collared shirt, with her hand resting on his thigh, clad in light blue Levi's. His glistening blonde hair hung long and straight. Crushed on his head a black and blue baseball cap with the word *Vampire* stitched across the front. That was what Luka wanted of her. Her life's blood, to be his, and though it should, that idea no longer frightened her.

Luka's hair lay intertwined with her long sable hair, representing her life with him. She moved her hand to rest over his heart. It was beating, easily, providing a soothing rhythm. She snuggled real close, comfortable, and grateful she and Luka shared a full and exciting life together.

But without warning, her emotions turned on her and flushed her anger to the surface with hot stinging tears of frustration. If not for the fact that Kaine owned her heart, she might be able to find contentment and complete happiness with Luka — for a lifetime.

I hate you, Kaine Walker, she said in her mind's eye.

The count was close, two days until the simulcast and

fifteen days until Ian's wedding. Holly knew Luka's only real chance with her would depend on what happened during her interview. She would have all her questions answered once and for all when she laid eyes on Kaine.

It was late when Luka kissed her at her front door with his usual restrained passion and she secretly wondered how he controlled himself.

Holly wondered how she had.

And she wondered if he hid a secret mistress or many one-offs somewhere high in the canyon or sprinkled about in luxury apartments.

Sometimes Holly wished he would permit himself to let go and allow her to feel him — wild and alive once again as she had that fateful day in Malibu. She was positive Luka would prove to be a better lover than the spiteful Tessa led her to believe.

But for Luka to love her with more passion than Kaine, might turn out to be impossible. The question — would she ever find out?

Her thoughts revolved around the two most desirable men on the planet, and here she sat, alone again!

Holly walked in her cottage and turned up the thermostat as she checked for the blinking light on her message machine. As she reached to replay her days' worth of messages, the recorder clicked on startling her. With the ringer turned off because of the late hour, she waited to screen the call.

"Holly, Emily calling. I'm sorry..."

But that was all Emily said as Holly lunged to pick up the receiver.

"Emily, I'm relieved to hear your voice. It's been too

long. How are you? How did it go?"

After a moment's pause, Holly uttered.

"How is he?"

"I'm all right, and everything went better than expected. And, Holly I'm encouraged. Kaine's going to recover.

"And best yet, Kaine's been asking about you."

Chapter Four

THOUGHTS AND WORDS

Emily spoke apologetically, "I'm sorry I haven't called. The security around Kaine has been incredibly tight. Thankfully, Nicky decided to stay with me, or I wouldn't have been able to communicate with him either. That's how bloody well secretive Kaine's hospitalization has been kept. It wouldn't do to have the rock icon in for drugs in this era of safe sex and the public's down on drugs. It's nothing personal. I assure you, Holly. All security."

Tears rimmed her eyes. She anxiously listened to Emily, hoping for the best.

"I understand Emily. I've seen the tabloids fighting amongst themselves trying to find your fugitive brother first. What a media circus. I know it's not personal. Please, tell me, what's going on, with him?"

Holly couldn't bring herself to speak his name aloud for fear of crying uncontrollably because he'd asked about her.

There was hope.

"It would seem my big brother has worked out most of his Briarwood traumas. I'm happy to be the first to tell you, Kaine is clean and sober and determined. I'm confident he'll stay that way. As I was saying before, he's talking about you. Better yet, he's keen to make plans to see you."

There it was again. The thunder of her love for him pounding in her heart, over and over, and the lightning struck bringing surges of love, as she squeezed tears of joy from her eyes.

"He's making plans?" She repeated in a weakened voice.

Emily's voice quieted.

"Yes. I think he's keen to apologize for upsetting you at Friar Manor. I'm hoping for a bit of a visit Holly. But mostly to hear you have forgiven yourself for your part of Friar Manor."

Emily hesitated.

It caused Holly to bristle with anticipation, at her forthcoming words. "It's been difficult."

Emily instantly snapped, "Tell me … you will see him?"

Suddenly, relieved, Holly knew she would find the way to step over the last hurdle of her shame and then volunteered.

"Oh yes, Emmy. Yes, yes, yes! Where and when?"

"At Solange and Ian's wedding, he's healthy enough to attend. He's been at Briarwood Castle, recording. He's written brilliant songs. I'm happy to see him creative again. On a more private note, he's missed his horses and his privacy. I don't think he realized the rock legend he'd become during his absence. He's a bigger star than he was four years ago. I think his current fame surprised him.

"He needed time to heal before the interview for CMT with you. He's strong enough to rejoin the world in progress. He tells me therapy was quite an emotional housecleaning, especially intense and left him feeling vulnerable. He was reluctant at first to have to face the harsh and cruel world as a rock star. Well, put yourself in his place. Why else would he ask for you?"

Holly sat thankful for the inspiring words of encouragement from Emily. Healthy and creative, a Kaine, she met at the Hard Rock. There they'd met filming the first segment of "Now That I've Found You" — the day of their first incredible kiss — the day he'd awaken her.

Willing her joyful tears to stop, Holly admitted.

"I'm happy too, Emmy."

She caught herself. "You don't mind if I call you that?"

"No, of course. I hope you'll be my new sister-in-law soon, and Emmy sounds smashing, like family. That's what everyone close to me calls me anyways — except Nicky

"Holly, I believe Kaine is deeply in love with you. And I want you to know I have kept our bargain, against my better judgment. But I agree. You were spot on with your decision. Your news would have given Kaine strength to fight his demons, but this way he did it on his own, for himself. And he needed to do that. You're a strong lady, Holly. You could have lost this round and my brother too." Emily's voice dropped into a sad tone.

"It's sad he doesn't know he is a father. The news will make him happy."

Grateful for Emily's encouragement, Holly offered compassionately.

"Thank you, Emmy. It will mean more to me and our future if he comes to me on his own. We'll build a life together based on his love and respect for me, not because I'm the mother of his first child."

Emily quickly said, "I do understand. I agree with you, in theory, but it's been heartbreaking to sit and watch my brother suffer in emotional pain, knowing a few words will bring him ecstatic joy."

"Do you know the exact day Kaine will arrive for the wedding?"

"He's talking about flying out in time to attend the wedding rehearsal on December 30th. I'm leaving tomorrow for Colorado with Nicky. I will try to see you before Kaine's arrival, to fill you in on this missing time. I've more to tell you — my brother loves you. Hold on for a couple of more weeks. Your miracle may bloody well be on its way."

And changing the subject, Emily regressed. "I hear Nicky hollering for me. He's such a bother about me getting my rest. I'll try to call."

It was all Holly could do not to jump up and down right on the spot. Instead, she shrieked, talking to her unborn child.

"He loves me! He loves me!"

Emily's call arrived in the nick of time. She sat back thinking while taking a long swig from a mineral water. A talk with Emily always left her with more questions unanswered. But what was important, and what she chose to focus on, was that he loved her.

How did Emily know?

Had he told her?

And she found herself saying aloud.

"Oh Emily, I need to talk with you for endless days."

She needed to put her investigative mind to rest and let Lucy dig up the answers. Otherwise, this was the best news!

Kaine was healthy and wanted to see her. The CMT interview was going to be unusually problematic. To see Kaine without declaring her devoted love, and then the usual question popped up — what to do about Luka?

It was impossible to imagine what would have happened to her without Luka in her life. A protective and loyal spirit toward Luka swept over her, she would not have thought possible a few months ago.

Holly protested half-aloud, "I hope I don't have to choose between them."

With her next breath, she smiled, wrapped her arms around her growing child, and confirmed under her breath.

"There *is* no choice."

Chapter Five

STILL GOT THIS THING FOR YOU

That night Holly welcomed her dark-haired dream lover. She invited him into her bed, holding him, loving him as in London with no restraint. All the loving ways and passion between them remained alive as ever.

When she awoke the next morning, all that was missing was the heavy, lingering scent of Kaine's cologne in the air. She absorbed Kaine's heat all over her body. His sweet, oh, so sweet kisses aroused her, leaving her drained and in need of his marvelously warm body lying next to her. She'd loved Kaine with a radiant sense of renewal — hope for their future, something she hadn't dared believe since her first days with him.

She cuddled under her bed covers, gazing out the window.

"Kaine, Kaine, Kaine, the most beautiful name in the entire world."

Holly no longer feared reproach from her cheating heart.

She drifted over her agenda for the day. It was filled from early morning until late at night with preparations for her special guest, Sir Lancelot de *Hurrikaine.* She smiled, remembering the name she christened him long ago in the castle kitchen when they were falling in love.

Lucy's research proved invaluable once again by pulling up tons of information on the band's history. She finally held the encyclopedia on *Hurrikaine,* and it kept Holly enthralled until late each night. She sorted through all the press, videos, and interviews. But she found none of the answers to the ghost of Briarwood. In fact, Lucy dug up scraps of meaningless information on Briarwood. And Holly learned that live interviews with Kaine were far and few between.

Apparently, Kaine changed his approach to the media this last tour arranging more access to the press. For the past decade, he'd been a rock star recluse, enhancing the mystique of Kaine, and she felt Luka's handy work on that public perception.

But the research was a labor of love, and it pleasured her to be charting the historical map of her lover's life. Finally, she knew what everyone else did. What surprised her most was that there were no earth-shaking revelations as Kaine alluded to at the castle, at least not publicized?

I've done things I would never, ever want you to know.

Lucy submitted articles about the death of Kaine's parent's in the early eighties, but after that, his life reads like a rock music fairy tale. Precisely as he told her at Briarwood Castle. He'd indeed been raised in the Arizona desert with a country-western, singing mother. Her premature death when he was fifteen-years-old caused him to be sent to live with his estranged father in England. A father he apparently didn't know existed. It was reasonably tragic, losing a parent and then being sent to a stranger. But how many people, then ran into his good fortune?

Kaine's father was Edward Dunnehill the third, the Duke of Dunnehill. His wife Lenora bore one child, Emily Anne, Kaine's half-sister. No explanations were offered as to when and where Kaine's mother Anne and Edward met. Nor was there a mention of marriage or divorce. That meant they either never married, or the marriage certificate was missing. Interesting. According to the few articles Lucy could find, Kaine's father had a wandering eye for women beneath his station in life. But other than that, only a few articles contained facts on his father. She'd learned his father and stepmother were killed one night by an intruder. Emily had been the sole witness. And Kaine couldn't remember anything. Was this the ghost? This had to be it!

Of course, she reasoned, losing two parents in a short amount of time could trigger a life-altering trauma. But could it be enough to be the ghost, Emily, as much as said destroyed Kaine's life? The secret had to be something tied up with his lost memories of the night in question. She'd decided to assign Lucy the arduous task to find out.

Other articles spoke of Kaine taking over Dunnehill Estate. How upset the locals were when he broke centuries of tradition and renamed the estate Briarwood. He'd become Emily's guardian at a very young age and raised her, then in her early teens, which explained their unusually tight sibling bond. Kaine began playing in the local pubs, and his bio read like most famous stars, except in a few short years, he'd shot to global fame and became worth half-a-billion dollars.

Nothing after the death of his parents had been unordinary or traumatic. If one discounted the obligatory drug addiction suffered by the entire band. There were well-documented accounts on the rehabilitation for the band for the entire world to witness. Kaine's fishbowl existence had been scrutinized, and over analyzed by every rag and magazine in print. And this piece of news worried her.

Why would he succumb to drugs once again in London? She needed more answers. And, if he slipped once, would he do it again should the stress of the stakes became too high?

She knew the razor's edge always waited in the wings ready to claim her life when desperation swept over her. Were the drugs the same demon for Kaine?

Another thing that seemed to catapult Kaine a little faster into the limelight, besides his genius musical talent, was the way he'd turned his back on his royal duty.

Back then, every newspaper was running headlines about that. She saw Luka's hand in creating the vivid images. Kaine, the outraged American, growing up without the British sense of obligation to nobility.

The press loved how he turned his back on the aristocrats to become a rock star. That only furthered his legend with the younger generations, fanning his popularity as a notorious outlaw against the establishment.

Yes, that headline had Luka stamped all over it. Otherwise, nothing seemed to be too different from the other research she'd done on mega rock stars.

Yet there was something conspicuously missing. And the only way she could get to the bottom of this mystery before she saw Kaine at Ian's wedding, was secretly sent Lucy to England, on a bogus assignment. Then she could freely investigate without Luka or anyone else noticing.

Lucy certainly would uncover the ghost of Briarwood if she were able to move freely amongst the Surrey locals where Briarwood Estate was located. She would have access to the local papers and be able to interview the elders of the nearby towns. Lucy needed to find the truth. She would put Lucy on a plane tomorrow for England. Holly felt in her gut her babies' future happiness may depend on what happened to Kaine and Emily long ago.

Holly's head spun with too many unanswered questions. She laid her head easily on the soft Battenberg lace pillowcase, clearing her research, burnt-out mind. She replenished it with her treasured memories of her dream lover before bounding out of bed to dress for the day.

Dressing by morning's light, she wondered if Kaine dreamed of her loving his strong, masculine body, and kissing him all over his exquisite form. For the first time in a long time, she'd allowed herself to fantasize about loving his long, strong love with her lips and tongue. She enjoyed feeling the deep desires for him. Touching him, receiving his touch and most of all, the pleasure of him inside her. She dreamed of when she could open her eyes and hold him for real. Holly's loving thoughts of her dream lover called out in her mind to him, *soon my love, soon.*

She left her house and heard a few birds chirping in her fruit trees. The sky was bright, beautiful and clear only as Beverly Hills could be in December. All of CMT was a buzz. The reunion of Kaine with the Heart of the *Hurrikaine* was on everyone's lips. Her messages were piled high with reporters, each hoping to snag the exclusive interview. Her phone buzzed off the hook with the tabloids and magazines, firing a barrage of questions.

A few press hounds waited for her as she exited her car. She anticipated her house would be surrounded when she returned home. Ironically, she was scooping herself with her own story. She had no idea how anything would go. There could be no rehearsal via satellite. This interview would air live.

Lucy filled Holly in on Ian Montgomery's profile when she arrived at the set. Though she spawned dark circles from too many late nights, Lucy was ready to catch her flight to England. Holly hugged her, wished her luck and speed, and to expect a fat triple bonus for leaving at the holiday time. Her whole future was riding on Lucy's abilities to find the answers. Beautiful Lucy looked more like a runway model on her way to seek fame and fortune in England, not saving Holly's future.

Ian escaped his holiday commitments in San Francisco at the last minute, making the HHW rehearsal. Handsome as always, Ian entered, his usually long streaked blond hair, cut to the collar for the prenuptial. He was wearing a black tailored, silk Asset suit, with a light-purple, banded, collar shirt beneath it.

As her research reflected, Ian looked like he was from Northern California, a Marin County brat. The only son of a one-time, low budget, film producer, and his parents struggled for years, holding on to unprofitable vineyards in Northern California.

His father had been lucky to work with the creator of *Space Battles* in the early years. An executive at headquarters, Ian's father headed the special effects ranch, well known in Marin County. As a child, Ian trailed behind his father around the world while filming the famous, groundbreaking, space trilogy. His pampered mother was from old San Francisco money. She was a classically trained pianist and wanted Ian out of the rough and tumble world of movie production. She'd wanted to send her only son to study at Julliard.

On a freak trip to England, Ian was introduced to Kaine and John Roberts, at Kaine's prestigious eighteenth birthday gala at Briarwood. Then known as Dunnehill Estates. Ian confessed in many interviews.

It was that night, I fell in love with rock 'n' roll — Robert's and Walker jamming together. A hard combination to beat.

To appease his mother, Ian applied to Julliard. He was accepted. But much to his parent surprise and dismay, Ian simultaneously applied to another college of music on the east coast. After a long fight with his parents, they backed down and gave him one semester to try out the other college. That was all he needed. Ian learned early on, the heavy jazz-oriented college was not for him. He dropped out and accompanied his father on a movie shoot in London. And for the second time met up with Kaine. The rest was history. Ian didn't return to his father.

Instead, he moved into Briarwood Cottage and began to play the keyboards with Kaine in the local pubs. Ian was, indeed, Kaine's best friend in the world.

As Ian Montgomery approached her, Holly thought —

there's another famous and great looking rock star. His usually clean-shaven face sported a few day's growth of light, manicured facial hair. Ian stood inches away. Holly lifted her hand to stroke his beard. She smiled a warm, loving smile. Ian had done all he could to reunite her with Kaine. He was a good friend to Kaine.

"I like it!" She critiqued as he greeted her.

"Holly, thank you, good to see you. Say you made time for us to go to lunch after the taping."

"You took the words right out of my mouth, Ian."

Then he gave her a giant, sisterly hug.

She paused, holding him too long. But he was the closest to Kaine she'd been in months. It was almost like hugging Kaine.

She and Ian had much to talk about and little time.

The taping went smoothly, and Holly did wade cautiously into why Kaine's illness captured the world's attention. If he'd been any other guest, Holly wouldn't have let them off the hook as easily. She allowed Ian an eloquent way to dodge her questions. He was able to protect the band's secret about Kaine's drug use and give Holly a bit of a scoop, divulging all of Kaine's hospitalization. The exclusive was — there was no hospitalization. He'd been at Briarwood Castle all the time. This was news and surprised her.

Kaine simply went home. And that 'hide in plain sight' move ensured his location had been kept top secret.

Ian explained there had been rumor mills with sightings of Kaine around the world, but no one had been able to penetrate Briarwood's security. Ian assured the audience, he'd been in recent contact with Kaine, and he was well and would be ready to kick off the second leg of the tour in the States late next summer.

Holly's heart skipped, Kaine was healthy. And Kaine would be here in the States for at least six weeks to eight weeks for the American tour. There was a time, but more importantly, there was hope. Though if the situation wasn't resolved, he would miss the birth of his first child.

She chatted energetically with Ian about his impending nuptials and his love of music. He shared his love for children and his fears about balancing his rock star lifestyle with his intended family. Ian was great. The only sore spot was the closing segment with Ian playing on his electric piano and Holly playing Slick. It was conspicuous to both of them who was missing as they performed "My Lady" with Ian singing.

After the taping, Ian walked up close to Holly to whisper into her ear.

"What are you planning to ask Kaine?"

Holly turned around and looked into the refreshing, jade green eyes of a man who had done his level best to keep her and his best friend together. *Bless him always*, she thought. But she'd no solid answers for him.

"I have asked myself that exact same question for two days. I have pages of neatly typed questions, but to tell you the truth, I haven't the faintest idea. As unprofessional as this will sound, it will depend on how I feel when I lay eyes on him.

"My Lady" racked up phenomenal sales, number one around the world. CMT plans to lead with both the video of the Hard Rock, and Briarwood. Both provoke powerful emotions in me.

"To see Kaine right after the airing, well, let's say that the world wants details about us. How can I ask him if I don't know myself? But that's the question everyone is waiting for me to ask, including me is 'what happened to us?'"

"You're right Holly. That's the buzz everywhere, and I've been on two continents. What about you and Kaine? In these dark and troubled times, your fairy tale love affair has captured the imagination and attention of anyone interested in entertainment. I must confess I'm right behind you wondering what happened to you and him."

They looked into each other's eyes. They burst into a howl of laughter. After Holly regaining her composure, she cried out.

"How silly the state of the world affairs are when anyone's speculating on my pathetic love life. I wonder what the odds are in Vegas," she added sarcastically.

Ian's eyes lit up brightly. "They're on your side by a hair. Luka's running close behind, and it might be a photo finish."

"Ian Montgomery, what are you telling me?"

"I'm telling you I have a lot of money riding on you and Kaine patching things up and enjoy the rest of your lives together. That's what."

Holly playfully slapped Ian on his shoulder.

"Vegas?" She laughed and shook her head.

Holly heard a loud commotion. Luka entered from the direction of the control booth calling everyone to surround him.

He always took her breath away, as she looked at him attractively dressed in a plain pair of dark 501-fitted Levi's, and a midnight blue, long sleeved shirt, under a black denim vest. His hair was tied back, and a black baseball cap on his head read TOM PETTY.

She hadn't seen him all morning and considering her newly betrothed feelings toward Kaine, she hoped Luka would understand her deep feelings of friendship and gratitude for him.

Whom was she fooling? How on earth could she ever, in a million years, explain to Luka, there would be no romantic future for them? He simply wouldn't accept it!

Luka's worried expression erased her rehearsed monolog from her mind. Something was terribly wrong. She feared the worst when he spoke.

"Holly, Ian." He acknowledged and waved them over to them.

"Ian, always good to see you," Luka said as he hugged him like a long lost brother.

Ian hugged him back as if there were no hard feelings.

Holly remembered how Ian insisted Luka be invited to the wedding and be one of his groomsmen. After all, Luka made Ian a lot of money and had shared the road together for over a decade.

"Stay here the pair of you, this involves both of you," Luka instructed, quickly waving his arms for everyone to gather about him.

Holly looked at a confused Ian, who shrugged his shoulders, looking as puzzled as she was.

Ian and Holly drew closer to join the crew.

Luka exclaimed. "We've lost Kaine!"

A hush fell over the gathering.

Holly instantly feared the worse.

Chapter Six

THE THINGS YOU SAID

Luka quickly continued. "Bloody hell, not like that!" He growled showing his irritation.

"Our London affiliate CMT-UK has a technical glitch with the new system. That's what those bloody sods call it when someone has fucked up in a major way. All that can be done is in the works. But, it's complicated. We can't pick up Kaine live. I had a chat with Clive, the CEO, and he hopes Kaine will agree to an interview in London. If he agrees, they will express the tapes at once, or transmit at the last minute if they fix the problem. No matter which format is used, we will edit it into Ian's interview by airtime. I'm sorry, but for the time being, the live interview is canceled."

Luka's Cheshire cat grin didn't reflect the sighs of disappointment from the crew. And it didn't come close to the heartbreak Holly plummeted through at breakneck speed. It took all the professionalism she could muster not to sprint into her dressing room and have a damn good cry.

Holly looked to Ian, who had his arms stretched out waiting to comfort her. Seconds later, tumbling into Ian's strong, comforting arms, she hated herself for what she was about to suggest.

"Could Luka have spun this into an awful publicity stunt to jack up the rating? To cause major international interest because I was going to interview Kaine?"

Ian was quick to answer, "Welcome. You're finally learning how Luka thinks. He's made the band a lot of money with less to work with over the years."

And quick to reassure. "Anything is possible with Luka. To be fair, I don't see how? It's to CMT's advantage to have both of you on screen live at the same time. That's where the ratings are. This setback may cause the ratings to drop a bit though I suspect not too much. It will be you and Kaine on the same show. That's news enough for most of the target audience CMT's trying to reach. And besides, Luka has power, but not absolute power."

How little Ian knew about the all-powerful Luka Hunter. He not only had the power if he wanted to discredit Kaine, but also this would be a perfect way. To let the audience believe, he wasn't well. Create more mystery to surround Kaine. She'd bet a year's wages Luka was at the bottom of this. And for the first time she understood how truly powerful Luka was. And that he was not to be fucked with under no circumstances. He could bring *Hurrikaine* down if he wanted. It would be easy. Stop the rotations. Stop the press, so to speak. Could Luka hate Kaine that much?

Holly clung to Ian's words, hoping he was right but aware he was wrong.

But she wondered aloud.

"I know you're right, but I can't help feeling disappointed

being kept from Kaine again. It's almost like someone is orchestrating these bizarre coincidences to keep us apart."

Her words rang true.

There was the niggling thought fighting to be acknowledged that it wasn't her fear of Sarah's threat that kept her from Kaine, but, somehow Luka was involved. His way of keeping her away from Kaine, keeping her close to him as he systematically ruined the *Hurrikaine* machine.

Was Luka that diabolical?

Suddenly she snapped.

Of course not!

Ian was right. Luka wasn't that powerful.

Ian pulled away.

He looked straight into her eyes and produced a sad expression.

"It is sad how bad things got after Friar Manor," as he let, go of her.

She felt a bit more assured, and Holly tried to assemble a smile, then remembering Sarah, inquired.

"Who had anything to gain by keeping Kaine and I apart? We're the star-crossed lovers everyone wanted to succeed."

Other than Sarah, there was only one answer to that question, and she saw the name in Ian's eyes, but neither of them spoke it.

Luka.

"I have something important to tell you. How soon can we leave?" Ian inquired cryptically.

The taping with Ian was flawless. Holly watched the replay satisfied with her questions that Ian answered with honesty and sincerity. She was confident her audience would see and feel her warmth and friendship with the most famous keyboard-composer in the world. Another successful interview in the can. It sat waiting for Kaine's sound bite to be spliced in with the rest of the interview.

The video and stage crews split up going their separate ways. After Ian had finished having his make-up removed, Holly grabbed his soft, talented hand and ducked out the side entrance. He had a secret, and she wanted to know what it was. They narrowly escaped the growing crowd of *Hurrikaine* fans amassed on the sidewalk behind CMT. Most gathered to catch a glimpse of their idol, Ian Montgomery.

Fans flashed cameras. And then the pieces of ripped paper, posters, and CD covers were flung in his face as his fans begged for autographs. Twenty minutes later, sitting in the back of a private restaurant in Beverly Hills, Ian ordered his entrée.

Holly lost her appetite. In fact, she only ate enough to stay healthy for her baby. She sat back waiting for Ian to tell her the news she didn't already have. Something she needed to hear from him alone. Instinctively, she expected Ian carried a message from Kaine. She stared into Ian's sweet, green eyes.

"Well?" She hesitated because she'd no patience left.

Ian wiggled in his seat, to get more comfortable.

"Well, I don't think what I have to say is a secret or come as a surprise." He locked onto her eyes and his words blew her into the back of the seat.

"I'm Kaine's best mate. I know him very, very well. Kaine's loves you. Probably always, will. There I've said it! The only thing I can't tell you is how long it will be before he does anything about it. I hope before Luka gets his hooks deeper into you."

"Luka? I don't...."

"Don't bother. I can see it in Luka's eyes. I see it in yours too. Care to explain?"

"Wish I could. But you've spoken to Kaine since he left the tour?"

"No, not face-to-face, I knew he was hidden away in the castle to throw off the press. He was shrouded in complete secrecy. Only the band was told. We didn't want the press to hound Kaine."

"I didn't consider the band having that information. Emily called last night and told me if Nicky hadn't visited her, she wouldn't have spoken with Nicky either. That's tight security, not his own brother-in-law, let alone his sister, could get to him."

Ian nodded in agreement as he flicked his long hair out of his way to eat.

"I don't know why Emily gave you that cover story. Nicky and Emily live on the estate. Nicky would surely have access to Kaine if he wanted. I do regret saying this — it's because you're tight with Luka."

"Luka? Why does that matter?"

"Holly, for an astute interviewer, you can miss the point. We could start with the photos — your show? In fact, how close are you that he gives you a TV show?"

"What are you insinuating?"

"Not insinuating anything. It's clear. You're Luka's girlfriend. But there are other things in the works that ought not to be privately discussed. Something's up, or I wouldn't be booked on a plane to England tonight at eight o'clock. And it's tough, with my heavy prenuptial schedule. No one seems to realize my parents are intertwined with Marin County society. I've made a social appearance every day since I went home from Europe."

"I had no idea you were such a dutiful son. Aren't rocker supposed to be rebellious?"

Was what she said, but that was not what was on her mind. She sat in shock, digesting the ludicrous idea that *Hurrikaine* believed her to be Luka's girlfriend. And Kaine must believe the same.

She smiled gently.

Ian sat quietly.

"Have I intruded Ian? I hope you understand that I would never do that. And, in a way, I can't explain, your family to me. And I never go against family."

Ian backed down, settling in his chair and conceded. "It's not that you have intruded."

Ian relaxed, and Holly decided it was time to change the direction of their conversation and asked.

"You were saying you're off to England. May I ask why?"

"Luka's sending me."

"Luka? Why?"

"I am needed! Why I have to be there is beyond me. Kaine, well, he can handle anything that needs attention. That reminds me. You slyly maneuvered us away from answering my question. What about you and Luka? The photos? Your show? How close are you?"

She reached out, covered Ian's hand gently, and decided to confess.

"I'm not his girlfriend, more to the point, we're not sleeping together. Anything more you need to know?"

Holly leaned back and sipped her mineral water while Ian shut his astonished mouth. His eyes said he didn't believe it, but if it was true, then why? He was puzzled. His eyes said they were trying to decide if she was lying to him.

Ian leaned back against the leather backrest saying nothing. His eyes studied hers, his facial expression tightened as his lips narrowed. Ian wiped the corners of his mouth with the cloth napkin and challenged.

"Well, it's my turn."

"Turn?"

"To straighten you out."

"I wonder if Kaine knows who he has in his corner fighting for him." She confirmed her compliment with a gentle smile.

"He's one hell of a lucky guy," Ian stated firmly.

Holly sat silent. She looked at Ian, who watched her process the compliment.

He smiled a full pin-up smile and then reminded.

"You're part of the family. But, remember, Luka always gets what he wants. And right now, that is you. But I'm rooting for Kaine. And if he's willing to talk and open up, I'll find out what I can, if you want. But Holly, I need you to tell me exactly where your head is, but more importantly, where your heart is. If I'm going to stick my neck into this and make promises to Kaine, tell me, which, by the way, I'm perfectly happy to do for the two of you.

"Let me turn the table again for a minute and put you back on the hot seat. Are you in love with Kaine? The way you once were in London?"

How could this sweet and gentle man question her adoration and love for Kaine? Certainly, he understood that Kaine was her life's breath, her only muse. However, his question knocked her off balance, shaking her reality. Did she love Kaine the way they once were? There was only one suitable answer.

Holly leaned in and almost in a whisper admitted.

"No."

Chapter Seven

NO ORDINARY LOVE

Ian's hopeful expression collapsed into utter dismay.

Holly quickly finished her sentence.

"Ian, I could never love Kaine the way I once did. I could never love him unconditionally that way again. Those extraordinary days lost in love in London can only exist in innocent memories. Since then I have lived a crash course in life's lessons, but, the love I have for Kaine is a newer love, a stronger one. Invincible I hope. A love that understands his humanness accepting he is a flesh and blood man, capable of making mistakes, as I have too, horrendous mistakes.

"Love Kaine? He loved me enough to forgive me for cheating on him with Luka in London. He's given me the time to overcome my hatred for myself because of my horrible indiscretion that crushed his heart. Time to see that I could love him again and not feel like I didn't deserve him. Love Kaine Walker? Yes, I love Kaine more than life itself. I'd do anything to protect and love him. And I know that if we are not able to work this out, there will never be another love as him in my life. They come but once in a lifetime and if we're lucky, we recognize it, tell them and hold on for dear life."

Holly experienced the usual flush of heat to her face, suddenly embarrassed by her strong revelation to Ian. But it was the first time she'd been able to verbalize how she truly felt for Kaine. The moments were truly cathartic in nature and thankful it was to Ian, she chose to confess her secret.

"What I'm hearing is, yes?" Ian replied, smiling, taking a bite of his pasta.

"Oh Ian, don't tease me. Yes, yes, a thousand times yes. I love Kaine Walker. More than I ever knew it was possible to love another human being."

And caught up at the moment, she leaned forward and cupped her hands around his, squeezing her hands tightly together for emphasis.

"In fact, I'm filled with a love that never ends and that made the pain of losing him too intense. I thought I'd lost my will to live. And for me, that was truly frightening.

"That's when Luka stepped in. His strong will forced me to pick up the pieces and build a new life. But it's turned out to be with him.

"And, I thought Kaine was gone, and Luka was here. He's been incredibly supportive and attentive. I must risk losing Luka again to try to reach out to Kaine, to love him again.

"But facing all of what I have to lose, yes, in answer to your question, I desperately love Kaine."

Holly sat back beaming, confident Kaine could slay all the dragons before her. It was simple. She loved Kaine, and he would love her in return. Isn't that how the fairy tale ended?

Ian finished his meal and settled in, waiting for the server to clear the table.

"It makes me happy to hear you care that deeply for him. It sucked watching my best mate wasting away for you, destroying himself a little more every day, blaming himself for forcing you away."

Ian paused and thought for a moment before continuing.

"Holly, I don't ever want to experience that again with Kaine. He's my brother. We've feasted on beans and caviar, shared pissed stained mattresses and feather beds, the best and worst of life."

Holly leaned in again, noticing a thin veil of red mist clouding Ian's green eyes.

He spoke affectionately. "I love the old bastard too."

"I know Ian. Kaine is the luckiest man in the world to have people like you, Emmy, and Luka, to love and look out for him. I have the same feelings as all of you. I want the best for him, and at this point, I believe I am the best woman for him," she reaffirmed.

"What about Luka? How deep are your feelings for him?"

Ian stared as if to read her every reaction to this powerful question.

"Too deep. I have to find a way to stay away from him. When I'm around him, I lose all sense and reason." She confessed with surprising ease.

"I'm glad you recognize his powerful hold on you. Luka's counting on that. I wish you luck, but mostly, be careful. Very, very careful. We are ALL familiar with how persuasive Luka can be. I've never known anyone to beat Luka, at least, to live, and tell about it."

She waited for Ian to smile at his tasteless joke.

He didn't.

"You're not serious? Murder? Luka?"

She was ready to laugh. That sweet, tender man.

"With Luka, anything's possible. There have been compromising situations and Luka's a powerful and driven businessman."

She shook the haunting word, *murder.* It jarred something inside of her.

She looked to Ian wanting to shake the thin shroud of terror threatening to cover her. To distract herself she impulsively spoke, "Ian, how silly."

Ian didn't respond.

She had no retort and changed the topic.

"If you don't mind, I'd like to get a Christmas gift for Kaine. Could I impose on you to take it to him at the castle?"

"What is it?"

"I'm don't know. I'll have to catch up with you before you leave. How long do I have to shop? This must be the perfect gift."

"Five o'clock is the absolute latest."

Holly agreed and leaning over, kissed Ian's furry cheek.

"I'm glad you trusted me. I won't let you down, Ian. I'll meet you at CMT."

He agreed.

Ian, such a dear man to protect Kaine all these months. His words brought new hope to root in her heart. Following the optimistic feeling, she decided to find a gift for Kaine, something that would express her new found hope for reconciliation.

What could it be?

The closest shopping area was Rodeo Drive. Holly

wandered up and down, peering into the shops. She stopped in Guess and looked at clothes.

No, not personal enough.

Holly looked at Gucci and sniffed the colognes at Hermes but nothing came close to the personal blend he wore that drove her crazy. She stopped in a small out of the way store El Vaquero and admired the fancy boots, but nothing was as special as Kaine's custom footwear.

What to buy the man who owned everything?

She wandered around the tiny mall at Number Two Rodeo, over the inlaid brick street and stopped in the new shops. She noticed an Asset boutique recently opened upstairs. Soon she would need to go to the internationally famous designer's shop for the final fitting of the bridesmaid's gown.

Recent research told Holly, Asset created a couture clothing line exclusively for Kaine, and band costumes for the world tours. Following the first music video, Solange became a spokeswoman for the clothing line.

Holly thought to stop in and ask for an idea for a gift for Kaine. Then thought better. This needed to come from her heart.

There were only a handful of the shops that were decorated with the season's greetings as she continued her quest. She passed David Orgell, making a note to stop in for a wedding gift for her two special friends.

Onward she forged when she thought of jewelry she realized she should have stopped in at Tiffany and Co. back at Number Two. She surely would have found something there.

She turned to go back when her eye caught a glimpse of a shiny, gold, identification bracelet in Cartier's window.

Holly promptly went in as her time was running out. She spoke with the salesperson and selected a gold I.D. bracelet.

It would bust her existing credit limit, but this was for Kaine.

"Is there time to have an inscription engraved because I need to put this on a plane in less than an hour?"

"Yes, madam," he guaranteed.

"Great. Simply engrave."

… Your Lady, Now and Forever...

Chapter Eight

TIRED OF WAITING FOR YOU

Holly held the tiny gift. A powerful symbol of her renewed dedication to Kaine, and she tucked it protectively into her coat pocket. She hurried back to CMT where Ian promised to stop on his way to the LA airport.

She sat in the lavishly furnished lobby, hoping she hadn't missed him. Sitting back on the leather couch, Holly admired the white flocked Christmas tree trimmed with gold ornaments and white doves. She remembered how the interns fussed over the tree for what seemed like hours. But the result created an absolutely beautiful tree. She made a mental note to buy a tree soon. With all her work lately, she'd forgotten it was the season to be merry.

A white, stretch limo pulled up announcing a celebrity arrived. Ian rolled down his tinted window alerting Holly it was him. She dashed to the curbside and leaned in handing him a three-inch box that carried the message from her heart to the eye of the *Hurrikaine*. Holly hoped Kaine would be receptive.

Ian graciously took her gift of love, and she watched him

tuck it into his black Gree carry-on luggage.

"Thank you, Ian, for taking this to Kaine. I owe you a big one."

Ian leaned close to the window and smiled. "Make Kaine happy Holly, and we'll call it even."

Ian's window closed, and he sped off merging into the sea of red taillights.

Holly drove the winding road along Sunset Blvd., heading toward the canyon Holly secretly wished she could have inscribed the bracelet with her wonderful news —

We're having a baby.

There was hope in her heart, thanks to Emmy and Ian's encouraging news that Kaine wanted her. She was tired of waiting.

She placed her hand over her abdomen and rubbed motherly.

"Soon baby, soon we'll tell your father you're here."

The press was perched outside her house. They demanded an interview. What went wrong with the broadcast? Or, had Kaine flaked out? She ignored the rude comments meant to get a rise out of her to become the quote or sound bite for the next day. She walked down the steps to her small, crowded abode and realized how embryonic it was. But, it was home to her.

Holly stepped inside and looked around taking in an inventory of her upgrades. Especially, her favorite, a framed black and white poster. It was the current advertisement of her and Kaine kissing at the Hard Rock, and it was also the cover of the CD jacket. Luka's idea. To run publicity for both the band and her show.

Holly walked over and turned on her state-of-the-art entertainment center, placing a *Hurrikaine* CD in one of the slots of her carousel. She tossed in the videotape of Kaine singing "My Lady" and seconds later, his image popped up on her widescreen. He appeared life size. This added piece of equipment was a real plus. To be able to record and edit the film for the show, run videos when she and Lucy researched bands, and, of course, for her personal pleasure.

Holly ran a finger along Kaine's magnificently handsome face on the screen and promised.

"Soon my love, soon I will see you again."

Holly transformed her roll top desk to accommodate the fax machine linking her with CMT, Lucy, and Luka at the beach and at the Dream compound. She checked to pick up her faxes. She'd taken to wearing a beeper, and like Luka, attached to a cellular phone. And she couldn't imagine how she ever lived without her tech toys. CMT recently converted to desktop computers, another piece of technology she would have to learn to operate, and then have another installed here too.

Her new guitars hung on the wall. Below, music stands to rehearse for the closing shots with the talented guest. The rest was pretty much the same, except for the armoire. Bought to house her growing wardrobe consisting of spontaneous splurges and expensive Asset dresses and gown from Kaine and Luka. A housekeeper came in once a week to do the usual cleaning, plus laundry and shopping. Life was much easier.

Well into her third month of pregnancy, she was thankful the nausea, and constant feeling of tiredness mercifully passed. The only symptom she faced every day was outgrowing the lines of her newly purchased wardrobe. Holly had yet to show her pregnancy about her waist but had filled out with a roundness about her tummy. Her breasts were a full size larger and her nipples extremely sensitive causing everything they touched to make her feel sexy. In fact, feeling sexy was how she felt all the time. And being around Luka was not helping one bit.

Holly wore the loose, maxi-dress style in fashion. Therefore, no one suspected. But she couldn't ignore the tightness in her chest. She took her prenatal vitamins and ate what she needed for her health and her babies. She would wait for her next doctor's appointment after the first of the year to find out what else was needed.

Maternity frocks made the top of the shopping note when she turned her head, hearing a knock at the door. She hoped it was not a bold, pesky reporter looking for a scoop on her and Kaine.

Holly peered through the peephole and pleased to find Luka's kind and loving face. She opened the door thinking he was a loyal and true friend, always standing by her. She owed him the respect to tell him she'd made the final decision to announce the paternity of her child. She would wait for Kaine and tell him at the wedding set for New Year's Eve in Pasadena.

Luka didn't step in. Instead, his expressionless face alarmed her.

"What is it, Luka?"

"Kaine consented to do the interview in London. The rushes are here. My intern LeMar called me from CMT. I was down the street and thought I'd pop by and pick you up on the way to the studio. We need to get there quick and oversee the editing."

Holly grabbed her long, black leather Asset coat and Prada bag and they were out the door. Soon she would have more answers, see the new and improved Kaine Walker. Would his delicious blue eyes stir her as always, and his kissable heart-shaped lips drive her to want him then and there?

Holly had waited too long, and she couldn't wait to see her lover and father of her baby.

Chapter Nine

FROZEN

Holly sat in the dark screening room, anticipation quickly growing by the second. Any moment she would see Kaine.

She hadn't seen him since the rushes of the "My Lady" recording sessions. And those had proven to be an alarming tale of a broken man deliberately destroying himself.

Luka ordered the rushes to be shown in the CMT screening room ensuring Kaine would appear larger than life, like the movie star he should be. Nothing in Kaine's face or eyes would be able to escape her. The test footage passed quickly identifying the tape. Riveted to her seat, she closed her eyes. A moment later, she bravely opened them to gaze into the clear, sober, apathetic, Technicolor blue eyes of Kaine Walker — Rock Star — former lover and father of her child.

The shock wave devastated her fragile psyche.

Gone was the joy and passion she'd remembered in his eyes. She was stunned. The image of Kaine faintly reminiscent of the broken man she watched climb onto the jet in London. Behind him, hung a gigantic *Hurrikaine* logo. And all she could think of was the once powerful *Hurrikaine* sat destroyed. A raging storm no more, tamed to a temperate breeze.

Kaine sat before her, the reclusive, globally famous rock star. His attire announced he was comfortable with who he was. His beautiful dark, shiny hair cut much shorter. Gone was the romantic traveler look, replaced with a blunt cut to his collar with long sideburns. He wore no other facial hair, and he looked rested. He wore an elegantly tailored, dark, blue pinstripe suit, with a white collared, button down shirt. No tie and the shirt unbuttoned to the third button. It barely exposed his well-defined chest, she'd loved to caress, loved to rest her head on and count the beats of his heart. His ankle was resting on his knee. And she could see how the cuffed trouser draped off his leg.

This was a changed man. This was a rich, country gentleman, not the volatile rock star. Kaine wore no jewelry except the single diamond stud in his ear, the only link to the rock world. She hoped it was a sign to her of his continued love. Her hand went up to tug on hers. But most shockingly, he looked like a wall street executive, rather than an infamous music outlaw. Then again, she mused, perhaps they were the same.

Her heart raced frantically at the unnerving image of Kaine Walker. It was hard for Holly to discern what was different. Of course, the obvious, his clean-cut GQ look, yet something else was different from the things she'd come to know and love about him. His hair moved slightly as if feathers in a gentle breeze as he spoke. It prompted the urge to want to run her fingers through it as it beautifully framed his incomparably gorgeous face. Kaine sat relaxed, reserved, measuring his dialog word for word. His sentences were seldom more than three or four words. When he didn't speak, he didn't move, which distracted her more. What the hell was he doing? Who was this statue of a man sitting before her? When she stared into Kaine's black-blue eyes that captivated her and changed her life forever, she noticed they never blinked.

She carefully watched Kaine's charismatic image, as his lightly seasoned British voice droned on in an irritating monotone sound, answering the interviewer without life, without the passion she'd come to associate with Kaine. He never smiled, joked, or emanated any good feelings to interact with the audience. What happened to her magnificent Kaine?

Hot, stinging tears of despair, dropped and rolled down her cheeks, assuredly no one else was as disheartened as she was. But she once knew a man named Kaine. This image barely resembled that man she'd fallen in love with in London. Holly sat thankful she'd been spared interviewing Kaine on live television. Had Luka, known? Had he stepped in to protect her once again? She was not convinced she could have risen to the professional level required to camouflage her undeniable feelings of remorse and sorrow. Some way for the Heart of the *Hurrikaine* to react.

Holly looked over to Luka. He'd known, she'd bet on it. She thought she might have overreacted again, by sending Kaine the I.D. bracelet, especially with the heartfelt inscription. She didn't know if she could be his lady, or forever. Thoughts spun out of control, then suddenly made a sharp turn. What if the reason Kaine wanted to see her was to say goodbye, he'd had enough? Then again, what if he were to seek reconciliation with her and she said no?

He'd scared her again. She was not altogether positive she would tell him he was a father. Once again, stable and reliable Luka may be the only choice.

Her head was swimming, her heart hurt, and she heard herself whispering.

"My dear sweet Kaine, what has become of you? Will I ever find you again?"

Chapter Ten

STAND

Holly couldn't do it! She was sure she could not sit and watch innumerable showings of Kaine's taped interview, editing it into her segment with Ian. She would turn the entire project over to Luka once again to clean up, expecting that he'd never complain. Of course, he would understand that she couldn't bear to drift into Kaine's madness. Her pulse pounded, starting to grow into a panic because the house lights would go on at any moment.

Certainly, Luka and Michael would discover her teary, emotional reaction to Kaine. This would never do. She needed to draw on Kaine's strength as a professional performer to appear cool and aloof. She hoped she would fool Luka and Michael.

Luka burst in predictably, disturbing her thoughts.

"What do *you* say, Babe?" Luka would give nothing away in his expression either.

Lost for things to say that would influence her show, she weakly offered. "I, ... I'm uncertain? He appears rested, well?"

"Yes, he does. The country gentleman image is a touch of his usual brilliance. I'm wondering why he gave all those bloody awful monosyllable answers. He bloody well knows better. It makes Franks job harder though I'm convinced we can salvage enough sound bites to make sense and splice him in one way or another."

Luka's coldness didn't surprise Holly. This was business, Kaine was clearly a product to merchandise, and Luka was doing his best to make a rebellious and uncooperative rock star an attractive piece of merchandise.

Holly wondered why Luka was trying to act like there was no major change in Kaine. Was he like her? Or, did he simply dismiss the transformation in the eyes of the man before him? Perhaps he didn't give a damn.

With Luka, it was a hard judgment call to know exactly what he noticed or missed. But as usual, Luka, always astute, offered no opinion on Kaine's sudden metamorphosis. Perhaps he was familiar with this behavior from Kaine. Because she was convinced, it could never escape Luka's trained eye. What kind of game was Luka playing?

Holly begged off from the long night of editing with Luka and Frank. She quietly blamed her fatigue on the pregnancy. Then she rushed to her office and faxed Lucy a simple memo.

Hurry with research on Briarwood.
Trace Dunnehill name back three
generations. Urgent I find out what happened.
Time running out!

It was true.
She would see Kaine in less than two weeks.

The streets of Hollywood were blurry from her constant tears of mourning and regrets, and she couldn't remember the last time she'd cried that deeply since healing from the split between her and Kaine.

Holly desperately wished she could talk with Emmy, but she was en route to Colorado, and she'd have no cellular phone number to reach her. Ian explained at lunch that Solange was in Paris. He would meet up with her there after his London stopover, to fulfill prenuptial obligations with her parents while she incorporated the final changes on an intense investigative report she'd worked on for months.

And sensing the tide had turned against her, the burning question was no longer would Kaine return for her. But would she return to Kaine? With no one to cry to or confide her pain and confusion, her panicky feelings escalated. Her future appeared shaky at best.

She brewed herbal tea and force of habit compelled Holly to wrap herself in Kaine's letterman's jacket. She turned on her Hard Rock video of "Now That I've Found You," trying to make contact with the man she'd lost. She snuggled down underneath the sheet with her growing child, wondering if she'd been too hard on his father. Perhaps she misread Kaine.

Possibly, his reserved image was simply to cover his disappointment at a missed opportunity to see her. The fact that he'd not made contact with her made him appear cold and unreachable.

Holly drifted into sleep looking for her dream lover amongst the dark clouds in her head. It had been a long dark night. She didn't find her dream lover. He'd eluded her. All that was left of Kaine was his faint scent lacing the collar of his jacket.

The sun pushed in early finding Holly awake. She couldn't sleep peacefully. Dressed in a dark, rust, baggy sweater, black leggings, and black high-top boots, she grabbed her long, black leather coat and headed for a meeting at CMT. The clear, crisp, California morning failed to shake the cold and austere image of Kaine from her memory. His haunting facade clung to her like a dark shadow, and she wanted to run, run far away from Kaine, and never face him again.

Ten days until Kaine.

The countdown was close, oh so close.

Holly was grateful to be steeped in meetings, a lunch date, and research to keep her at a distance from Luka, occupied with editing the film. Luka seemed to honor the space between them. He hadn't given her much more than a peck of a kiss since the first night at the Dream compound. Most nights he would sit and hold her at the Dream, but no handholding, no restrained kisses. Nothing. The sparkle waned due to his long hours, and she'd felt the cool change.

That night was cold and lonely in the canyon. She'd almost succumbed to a contradictory feeling to call and invite Luka to lay with her in her bed, to hold her until she fell asleep. But she didn't because she wasn't confident he'd come.

The next morning Luka approached her, stunning as ever. He wore black Levi's, a black cowboy shirt, and a black leather vest. His blond hair was tied back and a cap saying Bon Jovi was crushed on top of his head. His charisma was strong and pulled her to him.

"Babe, I've been invited to a birthday party for Andrew

Wakeman. He's in town, and it would be good for us to attend together. Never know when the band may stop in town on one of their trend-setting tours. It could be helpful if you've met at least one of them. In fact, I'm trying to line up Andrew to come on your show. He owes me a favor or two though Andrew does anything he bloody well wants."

Slightly intimidated by meeting Andrew Wakeman, the godfather of outlaw music men, and a household name at her house, Andrew had always been her father's favorite rhythm guitar player.

"I wouldn't dream of missing the chance to meet a living legend. I remember him performing at Friar Manor. Fortunately, he was one of the few men I wasn't photographed with that night."

By early evening, Holly was dressed in dark jade, velvet, Asset dress that was draped to her ankles, with a low cut in the back to distract her hardly noticeable protrusion around her waist. She slipped into the black suede heels from England and sprayed herself generously with *Joy*, the perfume Solange insisted she wears to Friar Manor to drive Kaine crazy. It worked! Kaine went stark raving mad.

She heard Luka at her door as she picked up her black leather coat. My how things had changed as she looked up at the poster of her and Kaine kissing. She swelled with love, realizing she needed to stand strong and believe in her love for him.

"Be well my love," she said as she placed two fingers to her lips and placed her fingertips on Kaine's cheek in the picture.

Holly opened the door to an elegantly dressed Luka. A bit

too elegant for a rock music party, standing tall, and handsome in a black Asset suit, with a black banded-collared shirt. His hair was tied back in a tail, and his sweet, succulent lips were pouring out a barrage of compliments. "Babe, you look smashing! I must say for a mother-to-be, you're wonderfully fit."

"Thanks, Luka, I'm trying to walk that fine line between health, fitness, and complete abandon."

Luka drove high into one of the nearby canyons, but her confused mind was settled on Kaine trying to sort things. Luka used good judgment by not bringing up editing the piece. They had arrived in good humor before she knew it.

The hill-top house where Andrew was staying was rented by a record label executive and as expected, expensive and lavish. Introductions were made. Luka turned to have Andrew Wakeman slap him on the back, and the two chatted away, obviously old friends. When her moment arrived, Luka turned showing her off like a prize bull.

"Andrew, Miss Holly Hill. The lady I told you about yesterday. I'd like you to come on her show if your people can bloody well squeeze us in while you're here promoting your latest box set of songs."

Holly gazed into the kindest eyes, she thought she'd ever encountered, and Andrew's battle-wore face filled with a warm and wonderful smile. The gentle rock icon puts her at ease instantly, and she didn't notice where the time went. Thankfully, the party guest list was short, and she'd ample time to visit with Andrew on a number of occasions. By the end of the evening, she was confident Andrew would become her next guest regardless of his time constraints.

While driving home, Luka praised her.

"Babe, you're getting a handle on working people. Tonight, with Andrew, was nothing short of genius."

A shot of indigence fired from her.

"Luka, I wasn't *working* Andrew, as you rudely suggested. I genuinely liked him. He's unpretentious, comfortable, and down-to-earth. Who'd of thought he'd be such a dear and be willing to do the show this soon?"

Luka flashed his famous Cheshire smile.

"I did! As soon as he met you!"

The next morning Holly awoke wrapped in Kaine's letterman band jacket and once again, her dream lover avoided her. She'd hardly had time to think about the star-studded birthday celebration the night before because she inadvertently overslept and was late for the final fitting of her bridesmaid's gown.

Holly sped along the streets of Beverly Hills hoping the police would turn their heads and not give her a ticket for climbing well above the speed limit. She remembered the exact location of Asset, from her Christmas shopping for Kaine. She drifted into daydreams of Kaine receiving her gift. It was in his possession.

Had it softened the hard, impenetrable fortress he'd built around himself?

Did it linger about his wrist traveling with him everywhere?

Was she his lady *now and forever*?

Or, should she be sorry she ever sent it?

Why hadn't she heard from Kaine?

Or, was the answer clear?

She was not his lady anymore.

As usual, too many questions and not enough answers.

It seemed an eternity since Lucy faxed her with the disheartening update, nothing new learned. But she'd encouraged Holly that she was following a new lead.

Holly entered the designer salon and approached by a young, tastefully dressed young woman.

She politely asked, "May I help you?"

"Holly Hill. Ten-thirty final fitting. Sorry, I'm late."

The girl escorted her into an area that overlooked Rodeo Drive. Holly glanced down, noting all the hustle and bustle of the world's most expensive street, unaware and uninterested in her breaking heart.

Later, standing in her originally designed, floor length gown by Asset, she admired the royal purple satin dress with the black piping. From behind, she overheard the familiar squawk of a British accent descending on her. The voice grated on her frayed nerves like nails on a chalkboard.

"Look who we have here — The Mystery Lady." The words hung in the air more as an indictment than a compliment.

Holly stared into Tessa's flashing eyes. She stood tall and chic in a stunning white-tailored, Asset pantsuit, with matching leather boots. Her long, shiny blue-black hair flowed about her shoulders like a shampoo commercial and then down her back to her waist. Holly begrudgingly admitted to herself, Tessa was one stunning woman even if she did have the personality of a charging rhino. And for a second Holly felt a twinge of jealousy that this cool and abrasive woman had an intimate history with her Luka and Kaine. Yes, her

Kaine. But she couldn't overlook the glaring fact that she was Luka's wife!!!

Holly continued to look at Tessa, and she could see what attracted the two love interest in her life, her classy sensuality, and her teeming confidence.

Tessa sauntered up beside Holly like a sidewinder assessing the situation.

"Holly, what happened to you? Your one time, sleek line in this gown has been disturbed by this ... this ... paunch here," she laughed rudely and then pointed to Holly's thickening waistline.

Humiliated and ready to punch her once again, the young saleswoman interrupted Holly's thoughts by returning. She temporarily caused Holly to restrain her hands, keeping them from coiling around Tessa's long gooseneck. To defend herself, she glared into Tessa's haughty gray eyes.

"What possible interest is it of yours how my gown fits?"

Like the deadly snake, she resembled, Tessa was tightly coiled, ready and prepared to strike.

"Well Mystery Lady, unlike you, who flaunts her mistakes to the world, my creations are for impeccably dressed and pampered bodies. I can't have you parading about casting dispersions in my exquisite gown."

Holly's temper raged.

"Your exquisite gown?" She mocked. "What the hell does this gown have to do with you? Of course, how silly of me, you must be the seamstress?"

She'd responded, thinking she'd put this bitch in her place and twirled around to admire the lovely gown in the mirrors surrounding her, ignoring Tessa, satisfied with her acerbic response.

Holly's last remark obviously infuriated Tessa as Holly had intended, because Tessa charged over in a blinding rage, nostrils flaring and lifted the label from the back of Holly's gown.

"ASSET, are you dim? Ghastly researcher you've turned out to be! Where have you been living? ASSET! T-E-S-S-A spelled backward. My designs you twit!"

Chapter Eleven

THE BITCH IS BACK

Holly couldn't stop the scorching flash of embarrassment burning her cheeks, especially as Tessa bit deeper.

"Asset! Tessa spelled backward. I'm only here as a personal favor to Solange and Ian, who wore my first line of clothing. They helped to put me on the map and made me a reputable name, unlike you! Unless you like being called frumpy? That's who I am, Mystery Lady."

Damn!!!

Holly stood dumbfounded and angry with herself for not knowing this crucial bit of information. How stupid she felt being caught off guard, lambasted by this raging bitch. She needed to think fast. Her stomach spun realizing she was out of her element. Tessa had skillfully put her on the defensive. And the only graceful thing Holly could do was to retreat swiftly, lick her wounds and hope Tessa didn't love the taste of her blood.

"Look, Tessa, I'm sorry if I've offended you. We're going to have to work together on this gown to have me looking presentable to the world. But most importantly, we are both here for Solange. It's her day, and we both do want the best for her. Can we put aside our differences and make this pleasant for all involved?"

Tessa shifted her lithe frame uncomfortably. She lowered her tone of voice to cautiously guarded.

"I see why you have your own show. You're clever and have a talent for diplomacy. A smashing trait for an interviewer. I think I can tone it down a bit, but off the record, I wouldn't want to ruin my reputation as being caustic and sarcastic."

Holly laughed to release her building tension. "Believe me. Your secret is safe with me."

"Yes, I'm quite confident, Holly," Tessa replied, backing off, putting away her long lacquered claws.

They spent the next twenty minutes working on the waist and hemline. Then Tessa looked to Holly with unexpected, sympathetic eyes. She lowered her voice to a whisper and asked.

"Do you miss Kaine?"

Holly thought she'd heard Tessa wrong, Holly lifted her chin with a puzzled look on her face.

"Yes, that's what I asked you. Do you miss Kaine?"

Holly wasn't convinced it was proper to confide in Tessa, but what was the real harm?

"Yes. There isn't a day that goes by I don't wish things were different. Since you've asked me, let me ask you one. Fair?"

Tessa spread a smile worthy of any fashion magazine cover and then after a loud laugh.

"Haven't you heard? I don't play fair. You haven't been paying attention," she assured as she continued to laugh, then died down to a nervous laugh.

"But go ahead and ask. I'll see if I accept your dare and answer you."

"How does a beautiful woman like you let a man like Kaine go? Don't *you* miss him too?"

Tessa straightened her spine and looked calmly into Holly's eyes. But there was no defensive bitch waiting to pounce and draw blood.

"That my dear, are two questions. But I'll answer both. First, Luka needed me more. And yes, I miss Kaine every day too. And while we're playing girlfriends at a slumber party, let me ask. What's your excuse? Why did you let Kaine go?"

The question hit Holly hard in the gut. Answer simple. Because of her betrayal with Luka, and then the threat from Sarah. Holly understood she shouldn't have asked because the tables may be turned on her as well. Holly went over and took off the shoes pinching her toes.

"It's too personal to share with you, Tessa. Let's say we had a major difference of opinion." Noting it was wiser not to bring Sarah up at all.

"Yeah, I met up with a couple of major differences of opinion with Kaine too, called jealous and insane temper."

Tessa gracefully sat in a nearby chair. Her face softened, and Holly watched her fade into the past to reminisce, her eyes were laced with great remorse. Her face seemed to sadden at the thought of her past relationship with the strong and invincible Kaine.

"It was the end of the seventies. All had been well

between us for months. I assume like you, he treated me like his princess until his jealousy flared up at a birthday party for Luka. Then his loving fantasies with me changed to violence, and he was screaming at me saying I was making a fool of him."

Holly felt faint, from Tessa's latest admission, remembering his exact words deep in the corridor at Friar Manor. And the next few minutes were filled with finding Holly water. When she'd regained her composure, she insisted.

"Please, Tessa, go on with your story."

"Sounds like you've met the other Kaine?"

Holly shook her head in agreement. "Please, I'll have to trust you not to tell anyone."

"Trust me? No one's trusted me in years. I might like being trusted. We'll see. But, in an unusual twist, I can promise, you secret that is safe with me. And I am sorry to learn he hasn't yet overcome his violent temper. Anyway, he put me in hospital for a week with a broken jaw. Luka came to see me every day and Kaine stayed away. Luka said Kaine didn't want to see his dirty work."

Tessa took a moment to take a drink of mineral water. And that gave Holly enough time to remember Emily said the same thing about Kaine's father.

He kept Kaine locked up after the beatings. Didn't want anyone to see his handiwork.

How like his father Kaine was.

"Kaine kept telephoning and apologizing, saying he didn't remember any of it."

"That's the same thing Kaine said about our encounter at

Friar Manor. He didn't remember."

Had Tessa known Holly, she would have realized the expression she wore meant, she'd discovered another mystery. And she would find the underlying cause. Why doesn't Kaine ever remember these horrible incidents?

"By the time my stay was over at hospital, I was afraid to go back to Kaine, and I had nowhere to live. I wasn't making any money on my designs and Kaine had been a generous provider, mostly due to his first chart climbing songs. We had enough to lead an exciting, so-called life, with the up and coming rockers in London, at that time, and enough to keep up an unbelievably expensive drug habit."

Holly squirmed as she listened to a story too close to hers for comfort. Kaine had a pattern, a brutal pattern.

"Luka offered to run interference, explaining I needed to stay in London at his flat because of my injuries. He laid the guilt on thick though Kaine protested. Kaine had no choice but to let me move to Luka's. Luka was having a bad time of it after Carrin. And I don't think, anyone will ever replace Carrin in Luka's heart.

"My misfortune? I never left him. Somehow, later, we were married. Our marital bliss didn't last long. Luka and I didn't have the fire and passion I shared with Kaine to survive the touring and his absence for long periods of time. And after Kaine, all men pale — believe me. If I'd known that my life would be this empty after trying to find a man to love me like Kaine did, I would have gone back on my knees and found a way to make it work. Not that I haven't tried on several occasions, to rekindle the burned out flame with Kaine during costume fittings and such. But Kaine wouldn't warm up to me.

He took my defection and marrying Luka hard, unforgivable."

Holly's mind raced to compare her situation. Had she defected by going with Luka? Did Kaine feel the same way about her? Would he see Luka's becoming her personal manager and producer as betraying him again? Was this the time with Tessa, to try to find answers to the growing mystery of Kaine Walker de *Hurrikaine*.

"Tessa, did you ever go to Briarwood?"

"Oh yes. I lived in the cottage with Kaine, Emily, and the band for a long time. But the manor, Kaine would never let anyone or me go near that place. Said there was something evil out there. It had been Emily's childhood home. And if it hadn't been for his devotion to Emily, Kaine would have dumped Briarwood Estate though it was called Dunnehill Estate back then, even if he'd taken a loss. They use to argue about burning the manor to the ground. You'll be pleased to know I was upset when I saw the "Now That I've Found You" video and recognized Briarwood Castle. Kaine took you there."

"Well, yes. CMT asked Luka to hire me to do the shoot set up there. But Kaine never told me it was his home. I learned that from Emily, days later, after our difference of opinion."

Tessa sat down next to Holly, and sweetness accented her perfect face. Tessa wasn't arrogant. She'd created a hard, exterior shell to protect her feelings. After being with Kaine and married to Luka, perhaps she needed the facade to survive. It was sad. Would this be her fate? To learn how to cover her feelings as Tessa?

She placed her hand on Holly's as a sign of friendship.

" I've told you my pitiful war story what's yours."

Holly hesitated for a long moment, thinking that the secret of Briarwood was tangled up in the evil of the Manor. She would fax Lucy at once and have her focus her energies on tracking down information on the manor's history.

It was time to level with Tessa. Share her story of love and pain with Kaine. As unlikely a confidant as she might have thought Tessa was, the fact remained, she was the only one present. The only one to talk to, and of all people, perhaps Tessa with her history with Kaine, she would understand her continual attachment to him.

Holly listened to a loud roar from her empty stomach and suggested. "Let's finish this fitting and go out for a bite of lunch. And if you push, I'll tell you the whole sorted mess."

Tessa stood. "Better yet, let's go out to the marina and have lunch. You don't want anyone to overhear this."

Holly agreed. Tessa was aware she'd lived in the eye of the *Hurrikaine* and understood the press well. They'd love to get a picture of this, Tessa, and Holly together. By sundown, the tabloids would have them fighting and pulling each other's hair. They finished quickly, and Holly followed Tessa's brand new Mercedes to the 'boat' as Luka affectionately called it.

Holly didn't dare let on that the Day Dreamer had been moored in Santa Barbara's harbor the last time she'd saw it. And needed to be careful not to act as if she knew where things were located. It wouldn't do to rub her and Luka's relationship in Tessa's face that is if she wanted any answers. The link was with Kaine. He was their bond. Not Luka.

Holly felt out-of-place on the Day Dreamer as if an intruder. Months earlier, she'd been locked in Tessa's husband's loving arms. How would Tessa deal with her if she knew of their romantic escapade? The dreamy memories faded quickly as her head filled with her stories of Kaine in London, spending hours going through her time with him. The similarities between them were frightening. The only thing she kept a secret was the baby and Sarah. When she'd finished, Holly sat as stunned as Tessa.

Then Tessa warned, switching gears unnerving Holly more.

"Luka's had his eye on you since that first moment in Chelsea. He probably set you up to be with Kaine. No, don't laugh it off, Holly. Luka knows how to make things happen, the sensational headlines, the torrid love affair. You must be careful of Luka. I don't know if I've made it clear enough. Besides his obvious control-freak obsessions, he seems to have acquired an insatiable need to possess any woman of Kaine's. In your case where he met you first, Kaine's either too dumb or tied to Luka with a horrendous secret or management contracts, not to have been able to do anything about it. This will surprise you. When I first came along, I was Luka's girl. I left him for Kaine."

Holly gasped. Of course, those were the words Kaine used.

Are you Luka's girl?

And she remembered why Kaine had called her Luka's whore. Because Luka was married.

"Tessa, at this point Kaine's no better than Luka!"

"Hurray! That's what I'm trying to tell you. They feed off of each other. But of the two, Kaine is harmless. With his explosive temper and womanizing habits. As I said, I was

Luka's girl, and I left him for Kaine.

"It was such a tawdry mess for a long time. That was when Kaine began to warn me to stay away from Luka. I figured it was the old male competition too, but I felt it, Holly. It's deeper than that, and everyone connected with *Hurrikaine* has finally recognized it, but no one ever dares to speak to each other about it."

Holly could relate. She'd been privy first-hand. Only, times changed and people were speaking up, at least to her.

"Tessa I've been warned about Luka by Kaine, Emily, Solange, Ian, and now you. All of you have agreed on one thing — to watch out for Luka. It's hard for me to believe he's as treacherous as everyone makes him out to be. He's always been there for me."

"Luka's been there for all of us at one time or another. But the problem is later when he turns our blunder against us. That's when he is dangerous. All I can offer is Luka does appear to be more sincerely involved with you and is watching himself more closely than usual.

"The fact that he's representing you is a tremendous coup for you. He's been asked by the top performers in the business to take over their careers since he led Kaine to the top. But his answer had always been no. There was no amount of money he was willing to accept."

Holly needed to ask, already fearing the answer. "How many clients has Luka represented?"

"Three. *Hurrikaine*, Kaine, and now you. And knowing Luka as I do, there's every indication that since he's no longer distracted on the road, his feelings are running deep for you. After I take him to the cleaners, you can relax, he will be financially secure for the rest of his natural life, and for any family he may have.

"You, my dear, may have done something until these recent turns in events, I figured impossible.

"Luka may have fallen in love with you and won't do anything to jeopardize it. It's ironic that the Heart of the *Hurrikaine* whipped the omnipotent Luka Hunter."

Holly thought to herself, Tessa didn't realize how omnipotent he truly was as the owner of CMT.

"And for my money," Tessa continued, "I believe he will never have you. Not if you have Kaine in your blood as I suspect you do."

What an odd choice of words.

Have Kaine in your blood.

How close to the truth Tessa was.

"But be forewarned. Luka is vicious and spitefully cruel," Tessa pointed out, laying her delicate, manicured, fingertips lightly on Holly's arm.

"He will do what is necessary for Luka to win."

Holly didn't like the sound of that.

"Do anything? Why? What do you think Luka is capable of doing?"

"Anything Holly, anything."

Holly backed away. This couldn't be happening again. Ian suggested the same sinister idea.

"How far Tessa, tell me. Would Luka hurt anyone?"

Tessa came up real close for emphasis.

"Already has, but he can do worse."

Holly swallowed and asked, "Are you suggesting what I think you are? Luka would murder to get what he wants?"

Tessa took a step closer to Holly, leaning in real close, revealing her status as a true victim of the press eavesdropping on private conversations.

"I'm saying Luka is capable of doing anything if he thinks it will accomplish what he wants. He wants you.

"And to answer the question, yes.

"Luka is quite capable of murder."

Chapter Twelve

LONG, LONG TIME

The long drive home under a moonless sky from the marina passed quickly. But there's been ample time to compare all the similarities between her and Tessa's relationship with the magnetic and passionate Kaine, and then the supposedly dangerous Luka.

Didn't any woman get involved with just one of these men? Were they a package? But Tessa didn't furnish the additional names of the demons Kaine carried other than a temper and jealousy. Holly had met them both. Was Tessa aware of any more?

It would seem that as far as Tessa knew, Sarah, that red-haired bitch, Kaine's personal assistant, and vicious guard dog, suffered harsh treatment at the hands of the unusually charming Kaine as well. This meant Lucy needed to find out all she could on one Sarah Cromwell. What the hell was her story?

Holly knew one thing. She'd joined a private and exclusive club. The Black and Blue club. It started with Kaine and his beatings from his father. Then, according to Tessa,

Sarah, and her beatings from Kaine. Then followed by Tessa and her broken jaw, and she — kicked and threatened by Sarah.

And who was to say how many more?

What triggered the violent pattern?

Holly parked on her back street and hurried into her house to collapse on her soft, inviting bed. She was suffering from information overload once again. The mystery no longer, about how she much loved Kaine, but his history, of a man with a past filled with suspicion and mystery.

Holly wondered how three competent and worldly women, seemingly had an impossible time getting Kaine Walker out of their systems. Mentally and emotionally exhausted, Holly experienced a flattening of her emotions and didn't know what to believe anymore.

Holly lay on her thick comforter, wrapped in Kaine's *Hurrikaine* jacket wanting to drift into a much-needed slumber. She exhaled waiting for the familiar scent to wash over her carrying her to sleep. A lonely Holly stood at the edge of the fog, reaching out with her arms, inviting her dream lover to join her.

Kaine avoided her once again.

Later, after the uneventful nap, she lit a fire in the fireplace and a fat, vanilla scented candle, found a pencil and paper. She picked up the guitar and jotted down lyrics for a song swirling around in her head, describing her present state of mind. The title eventually made its way to the foreground, *Trapped in Love with You.*

The daylight vanished and was well into the evening when she finished polishing her new creation. Then she

SURRENDER ~ Affairs of the Heart ~ HOLLYWOOD · 105

decided to move on to giving her fan mail attention when the intrusive knock came to her door. She drug herself away from her labor of love and stood at the door, peering out at a gangly, pimple-faced teen on the other side of the door.

"Yes?" She questioned with a cautious tone. He could be a reporter after an exclusive.

"Delivery."

Holly saw the black guitar case in his hands and cautiously opened the door. She accepted the long, slender, black hard-shelled guitar case, wrapped with a three-inch gold ribbon. She tipped the boy generously.

Holly was surprised. What did the case contain? But the big mystery was the origin. She unlatched the lid and found ten American Beauty roses, fragrant and beautiful. She took out the small, two-inch card out of its holder and it reads.

I'm cold.
Alone.
I miss all of you.
Love forever, Kaine.

Chapter Thirteen

LISTEN

Holly stood frozen, mesmerized. Kaine sent sweet-scented roses and heartfelt words as an indication of his constant love. And one thing screamed loud and clear in her head.

He loves me.

The gift lifted her sagging spirits. For the first time in such a long time, there was contact with the man she truly loved. It was time. She needed to tell Luka about Sarah. If anyone could stop her and keep everyone involved safe, it would be him.

Alone with her erupting elation, her mind found it annoyingly difficult to focus on her fan mail that poured in daily to CMT, mostly because she couldn't remove the satisfying smile. The mail was from young girls who'd written letters filled with dreams to become a personality like Holly, others from young male admirers scribbling enticing invitations and proposals of marriage. Mobs of fans caught her outside CMT daily for autographs. There were few places she went anymore that someone didn't recognize and approach her. Chased by the press and her every move documented, she was on her way to becoming a popular Hollywood celebrity. But after what she'd seen fame due to Kaine, that wasn't something she wanted. Not that she would ever be as recognizable as Kaine, rock star.

Ironically, with all this new attention, there was no one to share her latest happiness — Kaine's gift. She wanted to kick herself for not getting Tessa's cellular phone number since She seemed to adopt the attitude — 'if I can't have Kaine, better you and treat him well,' becoming unnatural allies. There was no one to call. Everyone was out of reach.

She walked the length of her carpet, popped in a video of *Hurrikaine*, pressed mute, and put on the latest Marc LeRouge CD when someone knocked on the door.

"It's late, who's that?" She remarked to the image of Kaine on the screen. Yes, she talked to him all the time and then hit the off button. The image vanished, and she turned down the CD. She peered through the peephole with a prick of concern. The view was obstructed by branches of evergreen. Her heart raced with anxiety as she cautiously inquired. "Who is it?"

"It's me, Babe." The familiar male voice announced with an urgent tone.

Holly's stomach filled with butterflies hearing his voice. Holly opened the door to find Luka dwarfed by a tall, Douglas fir tree. Instantly, her eyes widen, and her heart raced. She leaned in to kiss his eager, puckered lips, tasting the season's flavor of peppermint. It had been too long since he'd allowed this treat.

"What are you up to, Angle Eyes?" She asked cheerfully,

SURRENDER ~ Affairs of the Heart ~ HOLLYWOOD · 109

glad to see him as he drug the heavy tree across her rug to the only available space, an empty corner in her tiny place. He propped it up, scraping the ceiling.

"What do you think?" Luka asked, firing a bright sunny smile, obviously pleased to act as chief elf.

How brilliant his smile glowed. She'd missed it and walked over while drawing in a deep breath, inhaling the familiar scent of Christmas pine. Instantly, she pictured Sheridan, Wyoming, and Luka holding her, cuddling by the fire.

"This is wonderful, but why?"

"Someone has to drag the season into your busy life."

Holly sat down on her bed watching Luka working on balancing the tree. How could those despicable things Tessa said be true?

Luka is quite capable of murder.

Surely, Tessa was acting overly dramatic. She didn't mean murder in the criminal sense, defined as deliberately using violence and brutality against someone that wasn't in self-defense. She looked at Luka's attractive behind, molded into fitted Levi's, and instantly dismissed Tessa's exaggerated warnings.

Holly didn't understand why everyone was paranoid. Yes, it was possible but more probable that Luka ruthlessly abused people in the business sense, taking Kaine and the band to the top of the music industry. Yet during her extensive research into *Hurrikaine's* past, anyone else who spoke of Luka did with great respect and reverence. Was their positive response out of fear of retaliation from him?

One thing everyone agreed on was his accomplishments,

his business deals, especially concerning *Hurrikaine.* Certainly, a living legend in the music industry, Luka Hunter stood as an imposing and powerful man, and to own the controlling shares of CMT, would be his crowning glory.

But to commit murder?

Whose murder?

And speaking of murder — when was the time to tell Luka about London?

Holly's feasted her eyes on his suggestive dark blue 501 Levi's as he flicked back a lock of his platinum hair that brushed his shoulders. He struggled to pull the resistant tree to balance. He pulled a plug hanging from under the tree and pushed it into the wall socket. The tree instantly lit up with hundreds of tiny white lights.

"Oh Luka, how beautiful," she exclaimed, surprised he took the extra step to have the lights working.

She looked at him and added, "As you are."

He smiled up at her then turned his attention to a few branches of the fragrant tree that were being uncooperative. They drew a string of obscenities that spewed freely from his mouth.

She tried to swallow a laugh. Instead, she distracted him.

Luka looked up and his beautiful, baby blue eyes, twinkled like the lights on the tree.

"Oh yeah? Miss Hill, what are you bloody well laughing at?" Luka rose, heading toward her. To tease her, he produced a menacing look. But she saw the sparkle flashing his eyes. How was she going to take that away from him? The way he looked at her with pure intent, always happy to see her. But he needed to know about London.

She took his hand and led him over to the two high-backed stools at the counter, separating her space from the kitchen.

"Do you want a cup of tea?"

He sat down, with a look of 'okay, you need to tell me something.'

She turned, took the kettle and filled it with water, but didn't set it on the stove. This was going to be hard because he never saw this coming. Her real reason for leaving Kaine. She took the requisite deep breath and looked up at him.

"Tell me, Babe. What?"

"I haven't told you everything."

"What is it I need to know? We are here. The show is going well. What else is important?"

Exactly like him to paint the brightest picture.

"It's about Kaine."

"Yeah, Kaine? You can tell me. What information do I need about Kaine I don't already have?"

"The real reason I didn't get on the plane to Paris."

Luka relaxed his shoulders and quietly.

"Wasn't it because you realized that Kaine was no damn good for you and was smart enough to walk away?"

Again, expected, him being negative with anything having to do with Kaine.

"No, neither of those reasons."

Holly walked up to the stool, leaned on his thighs, and placed her hands on them. She looked up to gaze into his eyes. They weren't happy and filled with concern.

She began with her meeting up with Solange at the airport. Solange explained that Kaine was a prideful man and wouldn't apologize, but she'd defended him saying Kaine had apologized with flowers and gifts.

"And he'd brought me this."

Holly moved away and pulled out the large box the clerk behind the desk handed her as she was leaving the London hotel. She handed the card to Luka.

Luka sat quietly reading Kaine's final pleas.

> *My Beautiful Lady,*
> *Please, wear this in Paris.*
> *Tonight is our wedding night.*
> *Don't let me leave without you.*
> *I'll love you always.*
> *Your only forever man.*

"You see, he overheard me tell you I loved you in the corridor before the elevator door closed. Downstairs he'd changed the card and already forgave me."

"Rubbish! He should have bloody well forgiven you. What did you do?"

Holly moved closer to Luka, rewarding his sweet response to protect her. But she wasn't an innocent in their break up and tried to explain.

"He saw us in the shadows. He saw with his own two eyes, me in your arms, kissing you blindly. He didn't see us in the newspaper photos, he saw us while we were kissing. And if you remember, he'd asked me to marry him a few hours earlier. The betrayal he must have endured, seeing me there, and with you. YOU Luka. I think he might have been able to forgive anything but to see me with you, pushed him that night. And all the cocaine and alcohol-fueled his heartbreak.

That was what was happening down in the horrid corridor. His heart was being crushed by me."

"Babe, you can't believe Kaine went mental because of you and me?"

"I do and believe that's what caused him to go into his deep depression in Europe. I'd remembered everything Luka. The memory loss I'd sustained due to the heavy drinking and drug use, causing the blackout, lifted by the time I arrived on the tarmac in London."

He sat quietly. He looked up, stared straight into her eyes, and stated flatly.

"Nothing happened between you and me that wasn't honest and real. I knew that night. You did love me. Remember, I told you everyone knew, but that you were the last to know."

"Yes, I remember. But if I'd kept my wits about me, I'd be with Kaine, married and we'd be happy, especially with the baby coming that he desperately seemed to want."

Luka stepped back. "What you're telling me is it wasn't because you *didn't* want to be with Kaine that you let the Super Star take off without you? And, it wasn't *for* me? What are you trying to tell me? Why didn't you get on the Super Star?"

"I didn't get on that plane for two reasons. And I'm going to tell you both because of how we are involved. It's time I tell you everything. Because it may fall on you one day soon to protect everyone concerned."

That got his attention.

"The first reason you know. After I got over my shock from escaping the corridor, remember how CMT wanted me to do that last interview with Kaine. Only I couldn't face him. I was filled with guilt, shame, and betrayal. I was reeling from how hard he took my being with you. I hated myself. I didn't feel I was good for either of you."

"But Babe, we've discussed all of this. I'd hoped you'd found peace with what has happened. It's all in the past — ancient history."

"Not anymore. Kaine is coming for the wedding. I will see him. I have moments I believe I can look him square in the eyes, others not, but one thing is certain. I will see Kaine. He loves me, wants me. I can't predict how I will feel?"

She'd already decided her surrender to Kaine would have to come in small doses.

"Apparently, you have come to terms with the first reason, does that mean the second reason hasn't been removed?"

"It means, that with the second one removed, there will be a different outcome."

"What could make you reunite with Kaine?"

"If I knew his life didn't depend on my staying away." There she'd said it.

Luka sat quietly again. He was processing her dramatic conclusion.

"What does your relationship with Kaine have to do with safety? We placed security close to you and him anywhere you went in London. The hotel where the wedding is being held will be appropriately secured. Everyone's safe, Babe. Especially, you and Kaine."

She shook her head vigorously and countered.

"Sorry, but that's not true. Yes, your security focused on

any outside disturbance from the *Hurrikaine* organization that might harm Kaine. But you never looked inside the *Hurrikaine* family. And security never focused on me."

"Holly, what the hell do you think is going on there? Tell me!"

His voice rose, harsh and demanding, more than she'd ever heard him use with her. Then she was drawing out the sorted tale because she didn't have the slightest idea how to tell him.

"Let me tell you the way it happened. I was at the airport and once Solange learned that Kaine asked me to marry him in Paris, everything quickly changed."

She drifted back to those precious moments.

"Solange asked, 'Kaine wants to marry you?'"

"I'd told her that he'd asked me backstage at Friar Manor before everything went ugly."

"Her response was clear, 'Well, what the hell are you waiting for? He wants you to be his wife. Come on honey, you have a private plane to catch. Now!'

"Solange grabbed my hand and led me down onto the slick tarmac. I let go of Solange, hoping I would catch the plane before the hatch door closed. Then I unexpectedly saw Sarah, up ahead — Sarah — I suddenly remembered everything that happened at Friar Manor. It was Sarah. She threatened me in the corridor. I looked at Sarah. She is malicious and deadly. Then I remembered what you said to me."

"Me, what did I say?" Luka's eyebrows wrinkled his forehead.

"Don't let Kaine, or me, or anyone else make up your

mind. You're strong, you can do this."

"Babe, I didn't mean that!"

"I understand. You didn't expect me to choose then to remember your wise words. But your inspirational verse guided me in that all-important moment when I saw Kaine with Sarah helping him climb the stairs.

"Solange was visibly upset I stopped and was yelling.

'Come on Holly. You're going to miss the damn plane. Kaine will go to Paris alone.'

"But all I saw was Sarah. And I understood then. I understood the unvarnished truth of my feelings, my love. I needed to protect the one and only man I truly loved. I was strong, and I would let Kaine go… to keep him safe.

Solange was yelling to remind me that the plane was to take off soon. That Kaine loved me! How I was the Heart of the *Hurrikaine*. And that I would never find a man like him to love me as he did. She wanted me on that plane. But I'd told her it was too late for Kaine and me."

The memory rose, bringing fresh, hot stinging tears to lodge behind her eyes. The torment of that morning followed. Her shattered and exhausted soul left grief-stricken, her heart splintering into millions of pieces, shoving her to her knees as she finally let go of Kaine.

Holly wiped away her tears and added, "I told Kaine good-bye. Understand Luka, I needed to set him free because I'd remembered exactly, every despicable detail of what happened down in that corridor.

"I hadn't seen the black, leather boot that crashed into my ribs, at first. I didn't see it coming for me twice with such force that it caused me to coil up into the fetal position stop the excruciating pain, but I did the next time. I'd tensed all my muscles hoping to stop the sting on my face from the gloved fist that made my head bounce up against the concrete wall twice. Each time sending a fresh wave of stabbing pain inside my head.

"My clothes were ripped from my body, and then the strong, scent of roses filled the air when Sarah threw down the bouquet Kaine gave me on stage after he sang "My Lady.""

"I'll never forget those fucking, green, hate-filled eyes, moved closer to my face and her long red hair fell on my face. That was when I felt the cold nozzle of the gun pressed hard on my cheek, Luka. That bitch ... it was then I heard the hammer of the gun pulled back. Then the click of the trigger ... the chamber was ... empty, Luka.

"That's why I'm here.

"Her hideous words were spewed at me. 'I told you. You're fucking history bitch! Next time you get in the way of Kaine and me, I'll use this gun, and you can count on all chambers being loaded. I will kill you with Kaine's gun. If you know what's good for you Princess Bitch, you won't mention our little meeting here to anyone.

'Now, I've taken the clothes off your back so you have no way to go back to the gathering. Be the repulsive bitch you are, take these roses Kaine gave you and crawl back in the hole you came from. Or, next time you won't see me coming and won't leave you alive.'"

"She'd laughed and said, 'And with the way, Kaine and Luka have been at each other's throats over you, guess who will spend the rest of his miserable life in jail for your murder?'

"She was threatening Kaine, and she'd laughed again. And then her foot began to kick my thighs repeatedly. I don't remember what else happened, I passed out.

"I saw that fucking bitch Sarah on the Super Star, and that stopped me. I remembered every repulsive detail.

"She is responsible for my not getting on that plane. Otherwise, I would have taken all the love and forgiveness Kaine offered.

"I would have walked away from you and married Kaine, and I would have never looked back. But, because of Sarah, that's not what happened.

"And today, I'm afraid again. Kaine will be at the wedding as will Sarah. She is psychiatrically insane and dangerous. I'm afraid of what she is capable of, or worse.

"How can we play out this hand if Sarah ultimately decides? But I believe, there's protection because you have the true story of what transpired and that if any harm comes to anyone, you would have the truth and will act accordingly.

"I have stayed away from Kaine because I love him. I want to protect him. Soon he will be here. And I have been tortured, not being able to tell him the truth. This is entirely my fault!"

Holly barely allowed the last words. A moment later, Luka stood next to her, close, oh so close. His hot breath was caressing her cheeks. The peppermint scent made her head slightly dizzy from mixing it with the elegant perfume of leather that oozed from his black jacket. She sighed from relief, from not having to carry the secret alone anymore. But, this was not the reaction she'd expected.

Luka swiftly took her in his strong arms and spoke in a

soothing tone.

"None of this has been ever your fault. Listen to me, carefully. I will take care of Sarah. Put her out of your mind.

"Kaine, I'm glad he was right about what happened. He'd said he loved you. That he would never hurt you. For many reasons, I am glad that was true. He has enough on his plate without knowing that you didn't get on that plane because of Sarah.

"You and I? I'm glad you didn't get on that plane and not look back." He hugged her and continued, "I'm pleased you trusted me enough to have a word with me."

He pressed against her.

Holly took small steps backward until she brushed up against her bed.

Luka looked at her deeply.

She thought he looked through her.

He stepped closer, pressing her, and she fell backward onto the bed as the force of gravity pulled him into her arms and circled around to his back. She opened her mouth to allow a gush of air as Luka dropped on top of her with all his weight.

For a moment, time froze, as she stared into his gentle blue eyes that reaffirmed how much he adored her. Luka's sweet, hot breath surrounded her senses and a thunderous stirring bubbled inside her, gaining speed by the second until it shot through the rest of her body like a thunderbolt.

The last thing she saw was his eyes closing. The light brush of his eyelashes touched the high rise of his cheeks, before the taste of his peppermint lips fell wildly on hers, smothering her senses. His warm tongue swiftly entered passionately as if his future depended on it.

Chapter Fourteen

I'M LOSING YOU

Mmmm, *Luka.*

Holly relaxed, wrapping one leg about his. Her arms stretched around his shoulders, pulling him in closer. She began to hear her blood pounding in her ears. Her body was rapidly heating up as the lusty swirl began to grow deep below her belly. She was feeling the fire, the fire this man created. And she recognized this was irresponsible behavior and incredibly dangerous, allowing this man to pump her mouth, lighting her body with an explosive passion.

After her confession, this wasn't a surprise. The countdown to Kaine's return started for Luka too. Because now, he knew, he would lose her to Kaine. He'd seemed to want to make her feel safe, not hurt her, destroy her, and according to anyone near him — to kill, possibly her. She was thinking about Sarah and her hateful attack and the alarming confession about Kaine. She momentarily recognized that her internal warning system was sounding. Get as far away from Luka as possible. But it was too late.

Luka moved, sending his tongue deeper. The message

clear, he was going to both fight for her, and he was going to replace Kaine Walker.

Her last coherent thoughts were about knowing deep in her soul that Luka would never harm her. That it wasn't fair what the others said to her because he was the only man who made her forget Kaine. Powerful, lustful sensations overrode all her other thoughts of Kaine's return compelling her to surrender to Luka's delicious kisses.

Luka unabashedly kissed her.

Holly felt the force of the heat burn deep inside and her hormone-raging, pregnant body, was succumbing to the flames of yearning. She was close to relinquishing all reason because of the fiery desire careening inside her body at firestorm speed. Her breath slowed, becoming long and labored.

Luka was relentless, exploring her mouth, dipping into every secret place.

Her body responded, molding to his long, lean frame. The sensual scent of his leather jacket accentuated the sounds that ripped from his throat, his pure, raw maleness. He was luring her in, stoking her body with a fiery zeal. Soon, she would need to make another decision about her future with Luka. Her thoughts raced in circles. The delirium surfaced quickly, brought on by Luka's hot-blooded, passionate kiss. Holly forced her hooded lids open a crack to gaze into Luka's beautiful eyes.

He locked on to hers and poured out his love into her.

His brilliant love filled her quickly, and she gasped for another quick breath. She raised her hand, and her fingertips detailed his light colored eyebrows and long glistening lashes.

And thankfully, she saw no ghost of Kaine shadowed between them. What she saw was the exquisite face of a man who constantly proved he loved her. Luka's only crime was to make her feel wanted, cared for, but mostly loved, as he dropped his warm, tender lips on her once again. And his full succulent lips demanded all her attention and, predictably, Luka's strong magic made Kaine vanishes.

Everything became dreamlike as Holly wondered how dangerous it was this close to Luka, with the animal in him awakening and aroused. Holly marveled at how he'd been able to hold his forbidden appetites in check. She passively slid her hand up over his cumbersome CMT leather jacket, which served to remind Luka to pull himself free from it continually kissing, she lent a hand to help him take it off, signaling her willingness to please him.

She heard the jacket hit the floor with a thud.

He kissed, sucked, and pumped her mouth as if any moment she would evaporate.

Holly melted beneath his scorching kisses, sharing her need to be with him, and feel him — all of him. She struggled as her breath faded and she gasped, breaking into a pant. Her hips moved up to meet the growing hardness of him. He pressed her, setting his rhythmic pace, and she followed. His kisses moved to the beat of his powerful lust, and she followed.

Holly wrapped her free leg about Luka, nestling under his hardened sex, wanting him. She suddenly moaned aloud, from wanting to feel him, touch him everywhere. She fell into the rhythm with him, allowing her fingers to pull themselves through his soft, aromatic, silky angel hair. Holly wound both her lean legs around his a bit tighter, demanding a bit more. His opening heart was rendering her powerless to break the chemistry sparking between them. Out of breath, Holly slid her legs down and moved Luka to his side.

Her fingertips slipped beneath his shirt to trace his rippled abdomen. The hard feel of him made her hungry and flooded with the desire to touch his hot body beneath the shirt. She continued to suckle his sweet, velvet tongue. All the while, her breasts were responding to the tracings of his fingertips, sending her mounting swells of pleasure.

He gracefully separated her legs with his knee.

Before she sighed, Luka moved swiftly to place the length of his body next to hers like a handmade glove. Any inhibitions or lingering doubts vanished. It was time for Luka to make her scream.

Her hand deliberately went to the top of his Levi's. She struggled with the third button, then fourth and then slipped her hand deep into his private chamber, covering his moist sex with her hand. How long and hot he was. She did appreciate that he'd been in the right line when this part of his body was given out because she couldn't wrap her hand around him and touch her fingertips to the tip of her thumb. She smiled gratefully, anticipating the feel of him inside her.

After a deep, long breath, she set to work massaging, pulling and feeling his strength increase, as he pulsated in her hand. Luka's whole body fell into a natural cadence with her hand as he opened his heart to her, giving himself to her, letting her arouse him. His hands ran high into her hair, pulling her tightly into him. And she could not stop kissing him.

Wet and burning hot for him she was consumed by months of longing, holding back for too many days and nights. She hoped it was only a matter of seconds before she experienced his fullness.

Barely able to breathe, Holly broke the suction of Luka's provocative kiss. She dropped a string of feather kisses, down his hot, moist neck as she replenished her breath and intentionally headed toward her goal to please him, and she'd needed a deep breath for that.

She moved down, over his tight black T-shirt.

She moved, arriving at his beautiful, pink sex, surrounded by trimmed golden hair that seldom saw the light. She sighed. He was ready to astound her.

She paused for a moment.

The awesome sight of him excited her while the Christmas tree lights shimmered upon him as if he were a supernatural deity.

She moved closer to taste him.

But Luka wrapped his hands in her long hair and jerked her head back and trying to pull her up to him.

She glanced up into his smoky bedroom eyes and whispered.

"No, please. I know I'm with you. Let me do this for you Luka." Certain this time she would make no mistakes.

Luka's arms went limp. She watched him throw his head back into her fluffy pillows as if in agreement. His shoulder length hair followed the quick movement and came to rest, fanning across the pillowcase. He closed his eyes and parted his lips a crack for his quickening breath.

To bring him the same shimmering bliss he'd given her

was all she wanted. She smiled as hunger curled at the sides of her mouth.

He was waiting for her.

He would allow her to love him.

Holly felt his anticipation.

His strong fingers gave him away as he nervously twisted her hair about them. Then he anchored his fingers.

She meticulously, feather kissed his hardened shaft. She ventured to taste him, finding a hint of musk mixed with his sweat. Her tongue vigorously licked the beauty of him, with a frothy excitement. Sexy feelings detonated. She wanted him inside her. To fill her, pound her with his passion. Luka's moans said he wasn't far behind her in thought. She worked with gluttony and intensity that consumed her whole body. Tiny sighs escaped Luka's lips, and again he pulled her hair expressing his delight. Excited by his reaction, she let loose with her artistry, showing him her best talent. She wanted to taste his seed.

He softly warned. "... Babe."

And the idea inflamed her body. This was what she wanted. She ignored his warning to move away, she held on tightly.

The more Luka squirmed and pulled her hair the more she centered. With great determination, she'd decided to remain with him until he'd finished. A final inducement from her forced Luka's warm seed to burst into her mouth until he ran dry.

She laid her chin on his smooth, tanned abdomen, pacing her breath. How satisfied she felt, fulfilled, that she was able to show him a sliver of how he made her feel. She looked up to canvass his beautiful face and fell into the liquid pools of his angel-eyes before he closed them to accept the last sensation. How wonderful he was. Luka's chest rose and fell with a heavy, labored breath to match hers, as he rested regaining his strength.

Holly lay quietly by his side, guarding his sleeping giant that withdrew from his abdomen. It glistened from her mouth, reflecting the Christmas lights. His irregular breath relaxed and evened out. She submitted to Luka as he pulled her up his chest where he hugged her tightly. Her breasts were pressed against his chest, and she could feel his heart slowly briskly beating.

Luka pulled her closer to him, oh so close. Suddenly, he released her and sat up quickly. He kicked off his boots and stuffed his socks in them. He squirmed a bit more, freeing himself from the Levi's bunched around his ankles.

This was exactly how she wanted him, dreamed of him. Naked, exposed to her touch to ravish and caress. And there was a growing list of things she'd promised herself she would do to him the first time the opportunity made itself available. To taste his chest, nipples, ears, and fingers, to kiss him everywhere. Most importantly, she wanted to find out if it would be his name on her lips when she held Luka deep inside to make her scream.

But before she removed his T-shirt, Luka's strong arms drew her to his broad, masculine chest. To her delight, he began to undo the buttons that trailed to the hem of the green lace dress. His hair brushed her breasts. She began to assist him with her buttons.

Between kisses, he quietly scolded.

"No, let me take my time, I want to enjoy you."

Enraptured with Luka, Holly eagerly awaited Luka's skilled fingers. After each button, Luka dropped a hot kiss sending a clarion call. He was going to make love to her. Surges sparked rushing up and down her body driving her crazy with expectation. She was happy she'd worn this dress with a thousand buttons.

Luka damn near drove Holly out of her mind with delight. Each of his kisses slow, seducing, enjoying her, like cold ice cream on a hot day. He licked her, lapping at her flesh, making her burn. How long would he make her wait? Make her wait for him.

Luka moved one button at a time until he unbuttoned her to the waist. And like opening a present, Luka pulled her green dress open. He then unfastened her black lace bra that hooked in the front and freed her sensitive breasts to the cool night air. Her plump nipples hardened instantly. She was ready for his hungry hot lips to nurse her hard rosy buds.

His eyes widen, his desire flared, and they shined brightly in the tree lit room as he surveyed her breasts.

"Your body has changed. Your breasts are fuller. Your nipples are darker and plump, ripe to nourish life."

She raised her back, for him to suckle her.

He didn't disappoint her.

Ummm, how wonderful his warm mouth was. She was drowning in lovely rushes, and it was all she could do to remind herself, she'd have no protection, but protection from what? She certainly wasn't going to get pregnant. All that was left was sexually transmitted diseases and AIDS. As much as she trusted her life to Luka, she didn't trust him enough to endanger herself or her child by infection. She'd no idea where the incredibly sexy Mr. Hunter spent his nights when he was away from her. After all, Kaine called him a tramp! But it was as if Luka read her mind.

In a language lovers understand, he pleaded in a quiet voice.

"Please, let me love you, I won't enter."

The one thing she wanted most, out of reach once again. Why didn't she have protection? This must be a spontaneous reaction from him too since he wasn't prepared either. It took a few moments to relax, cover her disappointment, and trust him. She allowed him to kiss her one breast after the other, but there was too much time in between, he was moving too slow, igniting powerful feelings in her. He was pushing her to the point of abandonment.

He looked up at her.

"Tonight I want you to let go and feel me." He focused, kissing the curve of her breasts.

She lost all sense of decorum and wished to go crazy on him. All the while, Luka continued to circle her swelled breasts with the tip of his hot, wet tongue. He eventually zeroed in on her sensitive nipple, driving her into a raging heat.

Holly arched her back as he suckled her nipple. The feeling was exquisite. She hoped he would never have enough, never want to stop. His hand inched up her thighs, sending tingles to the top of her legs. She wished he'd forgo his promise and plant himself deep inside her. She wanted all the love he would rain on her.

Luka moved his hand, moving higher, up the inside of her

thigh, higher until his fingers rested inches beneath the elastic of her panties.

She yearned for him to undress her quickly. She wanted Luka in the worst way.

But Luka would not.

He would not be hurried, taking his time, moving only when it suited him and not a second before then. He must have sensed her frustrations.

He looked up into her frantic eyes and entreated.

"You're my woman, and with you, I will make love ... all night long. But you have to let go my beauty. Feel your feelings, the excitement, me."

Butterflies assaulted her stomach, his words heady, and a dizzy feeling swirled as if drunk and no warning arrived to stop her submission. How passionately he wanted her. Luka's sensuous touch set tiny fires on her breasts as she dropped a flurry of kisses on top of his golden hair.

Luka lingered, kissing her breasts until he satisfied his need. He moved down, down to the place where she carried another's child. He kissed the spot where her child grew. He lightly stroked her abdomen in a most curious way, respectful in manner.

Suddenly she was alarmed. Was she Luka's woman? Did she have what it took to become Luka Hunter's woman? Could she last all night making love with Luka?

Luka's wet, thirsty, kisses sizzled over her heated body, especially after each button, until he lay at her feet, the lace dress laid wide open. His body followed his hand up her body tracing the outline of Holly's high cut black lace panties, his tantalizing fingers ran along the inside. The tips brushed the scant patch of hair deliberately, to drive her frantic with wild lust and anticipation.

Lusty agony assailed her as she dug her heels dug into the comforter offering her hips up to his hand. She groaned deeply wanting him badly, remembering those magic fingers of his plunging deep inside of her.

Luka held back.

Did he want her to beg?

She would.

If she needed to, she'd beg.

She hated herself, knowing how quickly Luka could bring her into submission.

Luka masterfully removed her panties with one complete motion, all the way down her legs to rest somewhere on the floor. Umm, the night air felt exhilarating against her hot skin. She stretched her naked body, long and cat-like, posing for his approval, slightly separating her legs.

He didn't frighten her.

"You're a beautiful woman, Babe. I want to suck on the fullness of your breasts and swollen nipples. Your body is curvy. Your hips are slim and sexy. But mostly, I enjoy your willingness to let me love you — my way. You fill me with feelings I thought I'd never have again. Give me the sounds that tell me I please you."

His eyes were filled with the usual sparkle she was used to and grown to cherish. And as if he read her mind, Luka laid his cool cheek on her skin, near her quivering sex. He traced her hairline with his fingernail. Then petted her, he twisted his head and looked up at her with the clearest blue eyes to-die-for, and with his unmistakable sexy British accent declared.

"You're mine, Babe. This is mine." Then he carefully placed his fingertips between her lips to separate them.

She moaned, though he'd barely touched her, his words inflamed her.

The torture was unbearable.

He searched and then explored her depths until he'd learned what he needed to drive her to madness, bringing unending gushes of exhilaration.

The force of his penetration, stirred her juices, covering his fingers while she dug her long, lacquered nails into his hair with each intentional lunge of his finger. She wanted to reach for oblivion, and Luka sensed it, slowing his movements down, stroking her evenly and rhythmically, and then massaging her to the final point of exploding.

She'd guessed the purpose was to drive her out of her mind. No longer aware of anything but Luka, Holly craved all of him. And forgetting his promise, expected him to enter her, planning to feel his indulgent size filling her inside, pounding her, she blurted out.

"Please Luka, quickly, give me all you have."

But Luka wouldn't hurry. He'd want her bliss to linger.

She was unable to keep herself together. Holly's toes curled, her legs began to stiffen. She wondered how many more seconds of this unbearable sensual delight she'd endure. Wave after glorious wave, spread in her body like hot lightning and in a flash Luka buried his face between her legs, his lips hot with hunger and dedication she was thankful. Luka pumped and sucked, pulling moans from her lips and moisture from her body.

When she'd thought she could endure no more

indulgence, Luka's scintillating tongue separated her lips and as if it were his strong shaft, he plunged as high as allowed inside her.

Her muscles reflexed, closing her legs tightly around his head, as he willfully and aggressively pumped her. Her body trembled and shook, as she grabbed hands full of his long, luscious, silky hair with loud groans of gratification, filling her room in the canyon with the sounds of passion. Swells of satisfaction rippled, covering her lust soaked body. She marveled at the kaleidoscope of colors exploding like fireworks on her closed eyelids.

This was Luka aroused.

The only name that filled her room was Luka's, and she repeated it over and over to the only spectators, the twinkling Christmas tree lights.

Holly's handsome and sexy lover didn't leave her until she was satisfied. Many moments of mind-bending bliss later, she lay relaxed in a flush of heat. Every muscle drained. She was unable to lift her hands off his head or move any part of her heavy body.

He crawled up her steamy body to lay at her side.

Her only thought was to have him naked, desiring to see his luminous, golden form by the holiday lights. She wanted to wrap around him and hold on for dear life. She regained a bit of strength, but not enough to speak.

She tugged at his T-shirt telling him she wanted it off him. She drew him closer to her. His breath was pungent with her scent as she pulled his shirt from his back.

He lay at her side. Luka stretched long and desirable. Yes, he was a beauty. A wild, erotic, spirit dwelled in him, she was positive. But she dreamed of knowing his never-ending reservoir of passion that brewed deep inside him.

Luka leaned over and then sucked her nipple. He was slow, enjoying himself, lying perfectly comfortable in her arms, arousing her, creating new waves of shivers. He quickly alerted her body with a hopeful expectation. He may keep his promise and start again.

Reborn with an unquenchable craving to make deep love, Holly looked down to find his pink sex hard and ready. She wrapped about his body like a vine inviting him to enter her.

Luka moved in as well, separating her legs and moved in close, oh so close. He rubbed against her with his brilliant, strong gender.

Holly was excited, anticipating how he would blow her mind.

This was not the Luka Hunter Tessa cruelly described as a lissome lover. This powerhouse grew up since those days. Going around the world a few times must have sharpened his style.

This was Luka Hunter, her producer, friend, one hell of a sexy man and sensational lover. Holly surrendered every ounce of her loneliness and any lingering loyalties to Kaine. All the walls between her and Luka dissolved. She immersed herself in his robust desires.

Luka kissed her, his hands moved all over her body, longingly and bewitchingly, as he if he wanted to know every inch of her as if driven to possess her.

And she responded wanting to be all his as if buried in a fire and heat. Everywhere Luka's fingers touched, she reciprocated with voracious enthusiasm. There was nothing, she wouldn't do to please Luka. She wanted to care for him as he'd done for her all these long months.

Luka broke away.

His passion spilled over her neck and led him down past her breasts, down her stomach. Down to where she was certain, he smelled her, hot, wet, and dripping from his seduction.

She moved to caress him, but he flicked back a long lock of golden hair and whispered.

"I'm not finished..."

Chapter Fifteen

FIRE AND ICE

Holly learned many powerful lessons from Luka. First, he wanted her stripped down to her basic emotions. Second, he wanted to hear the sounds her body made. Essentially, he was teaching her to drop her inhibitions, to grow comfortable with the sounds of loving. She learned how physically strong he was, but most importantly, how strong his devotion to her was. Inspired, it was well into the early hours of the morning before Luka allowed her to rest on his lean, lightly freckled, sun-kissed arm. Obsessed with the shapes and contours of her body, Luka continually awakened her sexual fire making her insatiable. His years of experience on the road taught him a thousand tricks to delight her, without the benefit of complete penetration, and he'd blown her mind. Tessa's harsh critique wasn't true. One thing was clear, he delivered all night, exactly like Kaine, and he'd been masterful. Then the creeping seeds of concern sprouted.

Kaine!

Fuck!

Was this a grave mistake? To sleep with Luka,

encouraging him in an outrageously uninhibited way. Her mind was muddied, her body bruised and flushed from his intense loving. The clash of mind and body caused torrents of confusion. But her body was winning, screaming for more of his unquenchable passion.

"No, no more."

She'd heard him say.

And he seemingly withheld his sensuous touch from her like a cruel and unusual punishment. She'd lay obediently, stroking his naked body in the early morning's shadow. He'd taught her to follow her raw, animal impulses, and she'd let go, stroking him, adoring him.

There were niggling thoughts of Kaine fighting to return to haunt her, to remind her, he would arrive in nine days. He was fighting for her attention, her loyalty and presenting one hell of a dilemma.

What would be the outcome?

Kaine arrives, teeming with new expectations.

Luka, he trusted her, believed in her, clearly in love with her and most importantly, the man peacefully asleep in her bed.

All she managed was a hearty, fuck!

She told herself she wouldn't think about it anymore, being exhausted mentally and emotionally, but mostly sexually.

Holly drifted into a sweet, uninterrupted slumber, her dark haired lover banished from her kingdom of dreams, most likely forever.

The morning sun radiated in long shafts, between her blinds, casting long golden streams of light, reflecting her vibrant new feelings for Luka. She felt her angel haired dream lover touching her naked body, lightly in a playful manner, arousing her breath. She responded to his summons, delivering her body up to him to satisfy his decadent dreams. She moaned as she opened her eyes, to see — no one, the place beside her, cold and empty. She turned over and then glanced about the room.

Was any of it real?

Was it another torturous night of dreams?

No, there stood the Christmas tree, pungent, twinkling, and neglected.

"Good!" Holly exclaimed aloud, confirming Luka wasn't a figment of her imagination. This tree did arrive with the best present. However, she wondered if a hot night of loving lingered on his mind since he'd brought no protection. Or, he'd simply been caught off guard with her impromptu confession to loving only Kaine?

Because if Luka believed that being in her bed would erase Kaine in her heart — he was wrong. And knowing Luka, and how much he hated to be caught off guard, he'd decided to seal the deal with her by confirming she was his woman! He was undeniably in love with her though he'd never said it with words.

She rose and stood naked by her carnal nest. Where was the pile of clothes he'd left during reckless abandon? Luka — gone without as much as a word.

She looked over at her desk and saw a note.

B
Early meeting. See U straightaway.

No time to think.

She was due at CMT in forty-five minutes for a rehearsal and then needed to tape her show with Andrew. She jumped in the shower, and washed her sore and ravished muscles, singing a soft song while she touched every inch of her body Luka did.

Later, dressed in black lingerie, a long, white, linen dress, tight black legging, and two-inch black suede heels, she felt loved, sexy, and fulfilled. She sighed, and the spring in her step reflected a satisfied woman as she carefully climbed the garden steps to her dark green MG. Her hand flew to the place where her baby grew.

"Well, Storm, your mother's confused as usual. I hope this wasn't a colossal mistake. But I can't think about it."

Holly threw her leather jacket in the back of her MG and eased into the driver's seat. Pedal to the floor, she headed to CMT for her interview, but more importantly, she was anxious to see her beautiful and loving Luka.

Everyone was assembled when she entered the studio. Fortunately, she and Andrew arrived at the same time. They took the elevator up together, warming to each other. Andrew, eccentrically dressed as ever, wore a red scarf tied around his forehead, a white silk shirt with a cascading ruffle that billowed down the front to bleach-stained, black Levi's, and red high-top tennis shoes like a pair of Luka's. His face was rugged, but his gentle smile was warm and inviting. Andrew was animated, jovial and personable, a wonderful guest, a true professional.

The last half of the taping, Holly's eyes kept straying to Luka, standing regal and commanding in the control booth. He was doing what came natural, controlling. He was issuing orders and moving about the engineering soundboard with precision, punching buttons and adjusting levers. His only focus, to make Holly look her best. Her heart swelled with a searing heat and her sore body cried out for only Luka's touch.

Two long hours later, with her show in the can, was much too long to be away from Luka. She was hooked, and she needed his addictive touch. She couldn't wait any longer to be next to him. She sprinted up the stairs two at a time, almost running to the control booth.

"Hi, Miss Holly," Frank said, continuing with his editing.

Holly asked coyly, "Frank, where is Luka?" Trying to disguise the disappointment in her voice that he was not there.

"Upstairs. Michael called. Do you have a message for him?"

"Yes, please tell him I'll be in my office? I need to see him as soon as possible."

She tried to speak the words easily as nonchalantly as possible. She feared everyone noticed her new eagerness to see Luka and would confirm the rumor mill that she indeed slept with her producer. Holly headed for her office and didn't want to have to wait.

She was spoiled by his attention.

She wanted him.

Shame washed over her, because she wanted to feel Luka, taste the season's peppermint on his sensuous and talented lips.

It was happening all over again.

Holly sat with her temporary intern going over the next week and a half assignments. CMT would not be filming her show over the holidays, but she wanted to get a jump on the research for her next few guests. With Lucy out of the country, she struggled with extra work. But her mind was conspicuously elsewhere.

Holly heard her impatience muttered under her breath.

"Where the hell is Luka?"

Finally, the familiar tapping came to her door. She whirled around to find Luka. He'd found time to change. It certainly wouldn't do to have him arrive the next morning in the same clothes he'd worn when he'd left work. He'd shaved and dressed in a fiery red thermal shirt, like his unlimited passion. He'd thrown on a black leather vest and Levi's with matching leather boots, crowning his luscious head of angel hair, a black Stetson hat. His outlaw image left her breathless.

Holly moved swiftly toward him, longing to push her fingers into his long flowing hair and start loving him again. Yet something was different. Luka's eyes didn't sparkle when he looked at her. His cool, aloofness alarmed her. His voice was icy, then matter-of-fact, when he spoke.

"Frank said you wanted to see me?"

Thrown off balance by his frosty reaction she defensively reacted. Two could play at this, and she answered nonchalantly.

"Yes." And turning to the intern, she instructed. "If you have all the information, I need to discuss production problems with Luka."

"Absolutely, Miss Hill, I'll start working on this, and I'll fax you what I can find over the holidays."

"Good, thank you." But Holly didn't hear the intern any longer. Her thoughts were eating her alive.

What was her crime?

Why was Luka acting cold?

She hoped to ease the tension between them as soon as they were left alone. She planned to run into his arms and hold on for dear life. The intern bid goodbye to Luka and closed the door behind him.

Finally, alone with Luka.

Naturally, Holly was convinced Luka wanted her as much as she wanted him. That his usual English reserve prevented him from showing affection in front of the intern. She impulsively ran to Luka. She tiptoed up to kiss his luscious lips, those lips that knew how to kiss her blind and drive her body to oblivion. The same lips that kissed her body until she was singing in ecstasy.

She whispered, "I couldn't wait."

Holly waited for him to kiss her, touch her, drop to the floor, and repeat all the things he'd done to love her all night long.

But Luka remained detached and distant, becoming an intimate stranger. He stepped back, prompting her to lose her delicate footing.

Whatever she'd done, he wasn't in the mood to forgive.

Her condemning thoughts released the demons. What sort of fool was she?

She stood off balance, embarrassed by her adolescent emotions.

She felt the fool.

Holly ventured into the icy waters to ask.

"Have I done something, or, not done something?" the heat of self-consciousness rushed and scorched her cheeks.

Shame quickly waited to court her, forcing her to want to confess how she'd only wanted to please him.

Instead, she saw the hesitation in his beautiful blue eyes. The sparkle vanished. What happened?

"No." He hesitated again. His expression persisted unchanged. The face of an angel, but his words crushed her.

"What happened between us stays at your place, Babe. Nothing else changed."

Holly reached behind her to feel the back of her chair. She followed the line of the chair with her hand as she sank down into the cushion, into despair.

Luka sat down behind the desk and opened his briefcase. He pulled out the dailies for the Andrew Wakeman show.

What was this cold indifference? She'd never expected him to behave like this.

And like he'd never touched her, instructed.

"Go over these dailies while I'm gone. I'm going to be tied up with Andrew the rest of the day and tonight. I'm flying to San Francisco with him to film a segment for *Rock Live* before Andrew goes home to England for the holidays. I expect I will see you in a day or so."

Holly didn't understand Luka's dramatic change in attitude. Everyone had been spot on about him. She'd been nothing more than a conquest. He believed he'd snatched her away from Kaine once again. He'd proven that she would do anything he wanted, and his coldness and selfishness surfaced since she'd become the conquered pawn. He'd finally checkmated Kaine for a supposed crime committed against Luka long ago.

Or, was it simple? He'd come to realize that she'd meant

her words when she'd confessed to loving Kaine?

No, she thought not. That never stopped Luka before.

Her dejected spirit made it impossible for her to keep her usual effervescence on her face. She plopped her chin into her palms. She sat confused, and she was quickly trying to find the reason for his sudden change in attitude. She felt more stupid by the second as she watched Luka close his briefcase, stand up, and put on his long black, leather, trench coat. Only the tips of his Levi's and boots were showing. He turned and headed for the door.

Holly fought to stay calm, but the panic was lodged in her throat. She needed to say something. He couldn't leave her this way for two days. She'd go crazy with one scenario after another, wondering what happened. And then she would curse herself, feeling ashamed of her night with him. She rose automatically and magnetically followed him.

Luka stopped on a dime, turned to face her, close, inches away. He barely touched her with his provocative, tall, physique, towering over her.

She saw something in his eyes.

He was fighting with himself.

What the hell happened?

The knot in her stomach twisted.

This was torture.

She was overwhelmed with Luka. Then for a moment, for the first time, she found something in his eyes. Perhaps a hint of malevolence mixed with the growing sparkle in his eyes that oozed deep into her soul. She was drawn into his deep blue eyes, close, oh so close to Luka, and her breath increased.

Luka pursed his full sensual lips and slid his arm around

her waist as his lips crashed into hers. She took the full force of his maddening kiss. Before she got over the shock of her body against the length of his, she felt the steel plated armor rise between them as his kiss became one of his usual restrained varieties. But the restrained kiss was powerful, leaving her with the faintest hint of mint on her lips. Her head reeled, crying out with the injustice, knowing the possibilities of Luka's passion when it was unleashed.

Luka's kiss flushed Holly's face with lust and love. And when he let her go, she'd fallen limp in his arms, seriously doubting her legs would hold her up for any length of time.

He opened her door to leave and walked out into the corridor.

In her confusion, she felt drawn to follow him.

He took more steps away from her.

They were in the corridor.

He paused.

What did he want?

What the hell was wrong?

He stood there.

She watched him trying to decide while his hair was brushing the shoulders of the black coat.

He turned, set down his briefcase. He closed the distance between them with one-step and with both arms, pulled her into him hugging her tightly. He leaned her back a bit, to unbalance her, as his hungry mouth came crashing down once again, feverishly, possessively. His hands roamed freely over her body, consuming her, possessing her, branding her his. He made it clear. She belonged to him alone.

Holly was dazed, falling fast into a weakening state when

Luka chose to release her.

Then he picked up his briefcase, turned and sauntered down the office corridor, a man of power and influence, always in control and never looked back.

Chapter Sixteen

SABLE AND BLOND

Holly heard someone remark.

"What the fuck was that?"

As her vision began to focus, she realized Luka displayed his blazing passion for her in front of the entire executive branch of the CMT staff — for any and all to see. So much for the reserved English gentleman veneer.

His intention clear.

They were a secret no more.

Yes, it was true. All the eyes were focused on her. The eyes of the confused, eyes of the envious, and eyes that said the newspapers would know before the end of the hour that she was definitely sleeping with Luka Hunter.

Kaine!

That meant Kaine would know by tomorrow.

Of course, that was the plan.

Luka strolled beyond her range of vision. The office began to applaud their sensational performance, again catching Holly off guard. And the hot rush of crimson was on its way to burning her cheeks. She felt the thin sheen of perspiration flood her body as she thought quickly to curtsy to her gracious audience. She was playing the good sport and then she quickly returned to her office.

Yes, it was all a matter of time. The world would know she would never be the Heart of the *Hurrikaine* again. Her cheeks burned hotter as she realized the implication of her predicament. She walked over to the wall of glass and looked down to the boulevard. She watched the cars flow east and west, wondering where Luka's Jaguar was. Wherever it was, it was carrying him away from her.

She was alone.

She'd told Ian she wasn't Luka's girlfriend, and he'd surely carried that message to Kaine. After this turn of events, Ian would believe her to be a liar. And it wouldn't be difficult to anticipate Kaine's reaction.

Why did she surrender to Luka?

That question haunted her during lunch and the short meeting she sat in on to make plans for the next show. A half hour later, she was out of CMT for the holidays.

She was expected for her last music benefit appearance at a club in West Hollywood, and she needed to get home and take a nap. She smiled, thinking Luka exhausted all her reserve.

She walked in her house, and the memories of Luka slapped her in the face along with the strong evergreen scent of the Christmas tree he'd brought her.

She was surrounded by him.

Holly kicked off her shoes and put on an *Opal Pudding* CD. She conspicuously didn't turn on her video of *Hurrikaine*.

She felt like an adulteress again.

Holly turned the black and white poster of her kissing Kaine at the Hard Rock Cafe to face the wall. She thought to change the linens, but fatigue won, and she crawled between the crumpled and soiled sheets she'd shared for hours with Luka and inhaled his intoxicating scent. She lay remembering her long sable hair intertwined with his golden blond hair then drifted off to sleep.

The sun faded away. She awoke from a dreamless slumber. She grabbed cold, sliced, chicken, tore off a chunk of French bread, and opened a sparkling apple juice. She sat down to sift through the pile of faxes hoping for a word from Lucy.

But her concentration constantly betrayed her, thinking only of Luka, missing him, his touch and how their affair was a colossal mistake and could not happen again. The doubts wouldn't stop weaving throughout her thoughts.

Holly showered, left her hair to air dry into waves and curls, and then quietly dressed in a black velvet body suit and black slacks. She added a new black, waistcoat made of leather with beaded fringe. She popped on her new Tony Lama black suede boots ready to fulfill the final personal appearance that Luka booked for the year.

Holly threw the comforter up over her love nest. Turned out the lights and opened the door. Startled, she found the pimple-faced teenager from the previous night with a look of start plastered on his face. His hand held high, frozen, and ready to knock on her door.

"Miss Hill?" He said with recognition, holding another guitar case.

She tipped him and returned to sit on her bed and opened

the case to discover there were more American Beauty roses, each exceptionally fragrant and soft to her touch. This time, she counted — NINE!

With caution, she turned over the card and read on in horror.

For My Beautiful Lady,
Now and Forever,
Nine days,
Love Always, Kaine.

Chapter Seventeen

WALK ON THE OCEAN

Holly pulled into the alley behind the folk club turned heavy metal, then retro and then who knew what music wave? As usual, there were no surprises, all the evenings questions were about her and any chance of reconciliation with Kaine. After the CMT broadcast with her and Kaine, it was clear that, after all, these months, she was closely associated with only one man — Kaine. A stinging guilt flared, and a new sense of betrayal to Kaine assaulted her.

Why was Kaine doing this?

She knew why.

She'd encouraged him.

He'd received the bracelet.

Of course, that's why he'd said: *To My Lady, Now and Forever.* To let her know, he agreed. That he didn't merely love her but was coming for her, believing she loved him, and they would go away together.

Luka's powerful spell was dissipating, leaving her to read her own conflicting emotions. It was shaping up to look as if she'd made one titanic-sized mistake with Luka.

Or, was Kaine the mistake? Wasn't it Kaine keeping her from a wonderful life with Luka? The only man who'd been there with her every step of the long and painful months helping her pick-up the splinted pieces of her broken life.

That was a preposterous idea because if Luka never took advantage of her at Friar Manor, she'd be married and happy with Kaine at the castle, picking out nursery furniture and dreaming of their family.

Mixed thoughts of Kaine and Luka, continued to collide the entire evening. When she could take no more, she snuck out the back after her commitment was met. She idly drove along Sunset Blvd., blinded by her usual confusion. She followed the long winding road until she arrived at PCH, then turned and headed for Malibu — Luka's house. She walked up to where Luka showed her the hiding spot for the spare key, to use any time she wanted to get away. And get away was what she needed.

She grabbed a mineral water after she'd put on a heavy Navy Peacoat from the closet, she'd strolled up and down the moonlit sand for what seemed like hours. She walked until she could think no more about the pressing question.

Was it Luka?

Was it Kaine?

Not long ago, there wouldn't have been a choice or reason to wonder.

And here was the never-ending cycle, starting all over again.

Luka — a strong and dominating force, growing more important to her each day. She couldn't imagine life without him.

Kaine — with his strong love for her, awakened a host of personal demons. He'd done it all to love her. Loved her with the pure love, one she'd yet find in Luka.

And it was then she understood Tessa's assessment. Kaine's pure heart and love separated him from Luka. That's what made Kaine's love different. It was the smoldering look in his eyes that his love was true. How he'd given one hundred percent of himself to her, without fear, or thought to himself. And yes, he'd forgiven her, believing in their forever love again and, this time, there was much to lose by loving her again if she stayed with Luka.

Luka, one look into his electric, sexy eyes, persistently brought a tingle to her body. But with Luka, there was always the hint of self-preservation. That fleeting moment when she could see, he was protecting himself, always under control, and perhaps this was how Luka disguised his perniciousness. Was he an angel with a dirty face? Her usual companions, sorrow, betrayal, and ugly remorse filled her. Holly dropped to her knees in the sand and screamed to the stars alone.

"Kaine, forgive me."

The sun was rising on another day.

Eight days until Kaine.

Holly hoped she'd found a way to exorcise herself from the myriad of ugly feelings she carried. She needed a place to go where she'd not been with Luka to think clearly. The longer and harder she thought, the more she realized her whole life revolved around Luka. The streets, restaurants, CMT, the cottage, and lastly, but most importantly — her bed.

Luka was everywhere.

She stuck her hand in and struggled with the key to Allison's, her upstairs neighbor. She went up to sleep where Luka hadn't been. She needed to stay away from Luka. She didn't rest, more tossing, and turning. She was tortured. What did she do?

Darkness covered her when she awoke starve for coffee and buttered toast. She piddled around Allison's, but the need to eat won out over the ghost of Luka.

Holly reluctantly wandered down to her place where she found the third guitar case leaning against the door. She ran and picked it up as if it were fragile then quickly rushed inside and sat down on her rumpled, love-stained bed.

She threw open the lid, and eight long-stemmed American Beauty roses were thirsting for her touch. She anxiously turned over the card, placed her hand over her heart, anticipating Kaine's message.

My Lady Love,
Thinking only of you.
Your touch. Your taste. Your scent.
Eight days.
Your forever man,
Love Always, Kaine.

Chapter Eighteen

WHERE YOU GOING NOW

Holly sat with her roses pressed next to her heart. She described each and every petal to her son growing inside of her, recounting the love his father expressed for her. Kaine was showing his open, loving heart more each and every day. Her tears trailed, long and fast down her cheeks.

What did she do with Luka?

True, Luka was persuasive, but she'd fought the temptation of the sexy Luka. She needed to pull the pieces together any way she could. Kaine would understand the loneliness and abandonment she'd felt and forgive her — again. And that meant understanding *why* it needed to be Luka.

Luka, who Kaine understood better than anyone did. He would understand, he simply had to for their future.

The housekeeper was on vacation until after the holidays. Therefore, Holly began to clear the clutter in her place. The cozy nest received a quick once over with cleaning products until it shined. She changed the linens and plugged in the tree lights. She made a fire in the hearth, moved to the window, and sat with Slick working on lyrics to her latest song, "Waiting For You." A song obviously steeped in her present predicament. A bit too autobiographical, it made her squirm in her chair.

She abandoned the project, deciding to go shopping for ornaments for the tree. She stopped in at a salon in Beverly Hills. She decided to make a change and asked for eight inches cut off her hair to stop in the middle of her back. Then she added a manicure, pedicure, and a facial. Energized and renewed she was pleased most stores were open for last minute Christmas Eve shoppers. She picked up presents for everyone, including the special gift she ordered weeks earlier for Luka.

Luka, what the hell was she going to do about Luka?

Caught in the usual mire of contradictory thoughts, she realized Luka only achieved what she'd allowed. He'd always said no. He'd told her he wanted her and out of love with Kaine Walker.

When she'd confirmed she only loved Kaine, Luka changed his plan and went after her. Somehow, she would stop him if the situation presented itself again because Kaine was coming for her. Yes, her one and only love, the father of her child was on his way.

Out from under Luka's charismatic spell, with her head clear, her feet were firmly planted on the ground. She could only hope Luka would understand. Luka had been gone for two lonely days. He'd left no messages. Convinced she blew her business relationship with Luka, she'd finally resolved her conflict. She would tell him when he returned what transpired between her and Kaine.

At home, Holly found the expected guitar case for day seven. She threw her armload of presents on her bed and went back to retrieve the guitar case of love sent from Kaine. She pulled out a new vase she'd bought anticipating today's delivery. She opened the case and lovingly touched each of the seven soft and fragrant roses.

She hurried to turn over the card.

My Lady Love,
Thirsting for you.
Hungering for you.
Longing for you.
Seven days.
Love Always, Kaine.

Chapter Nineteen

NIGHT IN MY VEINS

Christmas Eve, and Holly Hill, CMT's newest shooting star and talk of the tabloids, sat alone in the canyon. She wiped away a tear after hanging up from explaining to her parents, visiting with her aunt in Maine, that the East Coast blizzards prevented her flight out. The cold loneliness assaulted her. It would be her first Christmas alone, but then she wasn't, she carried her most special gift for Kaine. And she dreamed about how happy her news would make him.

She set her packed suitcases aside, next to the guitar cases.

Holly finished dressing the tree, satisfied with the mood. It was decorated with natural ornaments. The limbs were wrapped with cranberries and popcorn garlands she'd strung to keep her nervous fingers busy. She'd turned off the lamps, to enjoy the twinkling lights, set the latest *Bon Jour* CD on random and nestled in watching the crackling fire in the hearth. She sipped warm, apple cider topped with a cinnamon stick and sat by the tree lit by the glow of the season. The rich scent of pine was intertwined with the battalion of pungent roses.

Her thoughts naturally drifted to Kaine, wondering how he celebrated Christmas in England, without Emily and then warm, happy memories of their love affair in London, washed gently over her.

The drawer!

Holly tugged on the square golden box, freeing it from the back of her dresser drawer, wondering if this was opening too many memories. Though she admitted, she was charmed again by Kaine's thoughtfulness, appreciating his exquisite choice. She placed the beautiful white silk negligee up to her breasts. Her hands caressed the soft silk with loving thoughts of Kaine.

She quickly donned a cap to protect her freshly cut and styled hair then jumped into the shower and washed off any and all thoughts of Luka. Afterward, she primped a bit lathering her feet and hand in scent lotion and then she ritualistically, slipped the floor length gown down over her head. And it fit her like a second skin. The bodice was filled, barely covering her plump, motherly breasts. The white silk hung, slinky and sexy. A diamond shaped, sheer lace panel covered her abdomen. She removed the sheer lace robe with nineteen forties style shoulder pads, the bodice panels were encrusted with handmade lace and with what she was sure were genuine pearls. She stretched her arms into the sheer long sleeves.

Holly felt like a princess and exceptionally sexy, especially knowing Kaine lovingly thought to have it picked out for her, hoping she would wear it for him on their wedding night.

"Soon, my love, soon."

Holly felt loved and content again, and sitting in front of her festive tree, she wrapped the final wedding party, Christmas gifts, when the familiar knock came to her door. She glanced to where she stored six new vases in boxes, for the remaining countdown. She cheerfully opened her door without the benefit of the peephole. She was jawed dropping stunned because there stood Luka.

Oh, she couldn't see him, but she recognized the cowboy hat, trench coat, and boots. His beautiful face was covered by the piled of presents in his arms. She stepped aside as he managed the tall stack of bright foil-wrapped packages as he made his way in and then cautiously stepped over her Christmas wrappings scattered about the floor.

Luka dropped onto one knee and sprinkled the presents about the bottom of the tree.

When she found her voice, she asked.

"Who are they for, Luka?"

Pleased as a small child, knowing he bought them all for her. "They are for you Babe, of course."

His expression changed, and registered delight, finding she'd dressed provocatively.

"You'll spoil me." She threatened.

The hot glow in his eyes made her suddenly realize how scantily clothed she was.

It was too late! It was as if his eyes hypnotized her and the heat burned through her with swift cruelty. She'd never known a man could make love to her with his eyes, but Luka could and how. She found in his eyes, everything but what she'd expected. His blue, blue eyes, sparkling, full of love for her, trusting eyes that never expected her crushing news.

Luka broke the moment, dropped his cowboy hat into a wingback chair, and shook out his long luscious angel hair. He dropped his coat onto her floor with a thud. Wow, he was astonishingly gorgeous. And after this flagrant display of his sentiment, she decided to wait to tell him. After all, it was Christmas Eve, and a day or two until after Christmas, couldn't make that much difference.

Locked in a trance, she continued to gaze at her admirer, wondering why he loved her.

Then he spoke.

"As I thought. You'd be sitting all alone on Christmas Eve. Have you eaten at all?"

She let him see his concern made a difference she replied.

"Yes, a bite of breakfast, but I'm hungry."

He rose from the floor. Luka flicked his long hair back and headed for the door.

"I suspected as much," he murmured. He retrieved another large bag from her porch, Chinese food.

He took two long strides, coming up to her, so, so close.

His lips a breath away.

"Happy Christmas my beauty. I've been a bloody fool, and I've missed you every moment I've been away. But look at you. This is why I love coming home to you."

Home to you.

Home.

That's when she realized!

She'd been in a romantic relationship with Luka for months. They'd been dating and were having the affair. He'd been romancing her since the last night in London. He'd been continually asking her out and then took her to all the best places. There were glitzy movie premieres, glamorous A-list parties, elegant and quiet dinners, and exciting, top–of–the–chart, concerts. Of course, there was the 'boat,' weekend and holiday trips, and the intimate evenings at the Dream compound, or here, where he called home.

She'd become his mistress, a few would say girlfriend and others whore. That was why he'd called her his woman, to confirm it, because to him, she was and for a while. And that was what everyone else saw that she couldn't because she was blinded by Kaine. Why they'd been telling her to be careful because they saw, hell everyone saw, he already had her right where he wanted her.

They were aware of the signs of Luka in a relationship. This was their romance. She'd been dreaming of being with him and she'd already arrived, months ago.

How awful for him to learn the true reason why she didn't get on that plane in London? She'd crushed him. And she wasn't finished either. She would deliver the news that she was going to tell Kaine the baby was his. That was tantamount to breaking up with him.

She watched him realizing that was why he'd been fighting with himself in her office the last time she'd seen him. He'd decided it was time for everyone to see how he felt about her and he'd taken their relationship public, right there in the corridor of CMT. And whatever tortured him while he was gone, he must have come to a favorable decision to be here loaded down with gifts.

Then the new realization arrived. He wasn't fighting for her. He was trying to *keep* her. He was at his girlfriends, his woman's, his mistress's house, his home, and it was Christmas Eve. This wasn't a visit, he'd come home to where he belonged.

He bent down to press his warm, sweet-tasting lips to hers. In seconds, fire shot at light speed from her mind to her toes. There would be no rescue from this burning need for Luka.

No, not now.

She screamed in her mind and continued to press her lips. Lips seared to his. This couldn't be. She was kissing him back with the full force of her explosive feelings, his woman's feelings.

Luka's teeth tugged gently on her bottom lips, his hair swung about naturally striking her face softly, flooding her senses with his sexy scent!

It started again, and she didn't have the strength to stop it.

But she needed to stop!

What a silly fool she'd been.

Their relationship moved far past anything she ever imagined. And she figured resisting Luka's loving was going to be the hardest thing she'd do in a long time. In fact, her body was responding independently of her commands. Her leg was curled about his. Her arms coiled around his shoulders. She was immersed in his scent and devouring him. And oh, the sweet taste of him, she was ready for what was to come. She welcomed her nipples hardening. She squeezed the top of her thighs together, hoping that would stop the scorching need for him.

Of course, it didn't.

The flame burned hotter. He was going to consume her.

She shook her head and leaned back in Luka's arms.

He broke the kiss.

His eyes closed.

He savored the taste of her.

This will be impossible.

She forced her leg to unwrap itself from his and stepped away from Luka.

He shot her a questioning look. But he'd apparently decided not to follow his train of thought. He turned and pushed back a few of the vases filled with roses and then set the Chinese food on the counter in the kitchen.

"You're fighting with yourself," he announced.

"Fighting?"

"You look at me. You want me, but the doubts."

"I don't doubt you, Luka."

"It's not me. It's Him." He confirmed as he pulled out white cartons of food and stacked them like a pyramid. With the familiarity of a live-in lover, knowing where everything was to set up dinner, he took out the tableware and set the bar with two settings, moving another vase of roses aside. His beautiful eyes seldom left hers as he caressed every inch of her with his fiery eyes. His mouth was turned upward, wearing a sinfully sexy smile.

Oh, this was going to be impossible!

Holly felt the indicting words hang heavy in the air. Yes, it was *HE* that caused her to fight with herself.

HE was coming back.

HE would be here in a week.

Luka felt the change in the room, because he suddenly subdued his smile, put a lilt in his voice to invite conversation, not accusations.

"I fancy that CD playing. That reminds me. We could pop in the *Bon Jour* concert. It's the night before New Year's Eve."

She sighed, relieved to have something natural to talk about, but, unfortunately, the common talk would center on *Hurrikaine*.

"Sounds great, but that's the night of the wedding rehearsal and dinner for Ian and Solange. And don't you have Ian's bachelor party?"

"You're right. Sorry, I guess I forgot. Well, I can always sort out where they are bloody well playing next. I'll call Jaden and make arrangements. If you fancy it, we could fly to see them?"

"Jaden?"

"Yes, Jaden Moore. The lead-singer, an old mate. I haven't seen him in a while." Then the old familiar look flooded his face when he struck upon an idea. "Might consider him for the show." His look was serious. His eyebrows were raised waiting for her reaction.

Her view of life was shaken because Luka thought in such different terms than she did. Can't see *Bon Jour* in L.A.? Okay, fly to see *Bon Jour* wherever else they were playing.

Excellent.

"Sounds great!" She responded, shrugging her shoulders.

"Tell me when and where." She never noticed he was designing her future to include him.

Pleased with her enthusiasm, Luka smiled.

"Smashing, I fancied their last concert in the 'round.' *Hurrikaine* considered it, but the simulated hurricane opening the show made it impossible."

Luka's plan sounded wonderful. Naturally, though it was Christmas Eve, Luka was already on the phone to someone issuing orders. A moment later, he turned and smiled as if to say done. She wondered if he would want to take her after her speech informing him she was waiting for Kaine to return. How could she hurt him on Christmas Eve?

It was all too fantastic.

Unbelievable, she thought.

Kaine was coming, hitting her like a ton of bricks. No more fantasy, no more *Hurrikaine* jacket to bind her to him. No more video's memorizing his every nuance. She would have Kaine close, beside her, hopefully, to have and to hold forever.

But currently, she faced the always alluring and spellbinding Luka. And he wasn't going to make it easy for her because he was moving closer to her and she knew her worst enemy was herself.

She changed the direction of the conversation, not thinking clearly at all.

"I have something for you."

Holly pulled a tiny, gold wrapped present from a tree limb.

"It pales in the light of your Christmas spirit," she gazed into his darling eyes.

Mistake!

Holly saw how Luka wanted her. How he held his passion behind a thin film of restraint. Her eyes drifted down his sexy body.

Damn, he was hard.

His pants tight about his groin, she wondered how he behaved normally. She gulped and turned away, suddenly feeling stark naked, aware of his erection.

Holly knew that moment. Luka was never going to let her go to Kaine. She knew he believed she would never escape him tonight.

"Any gift from you will be cherished, Babe. You know that."

He gushed with surprising sentimentality and then leaned over and took her hands in his.

Her body responded with a knot tightening in her stomach, like a noose around her neck. She volunteered a weak smile.

He assured her.

"One day I'm going to give you a small box, and I hope you'll accept it with the feelings intended."

Luka was sweet-talking her. But he never spoke the words. Instead, he squeezed her hands in his and the heat was sparking about her. It ran strong, and she was positive it rushed from her fingertips into him as his eyes lit with intense lust.

Luka's breath seemed to grow deeper, looking at her. This was going to be much harder than she already expected it would be.

It was one thing to imagine telling Luka they were finished as lovers while walking alone on the beach and then quite another to be in the range of his persuasive blue, oh so blue eyes-to-die-for eyes. Especially, when they were filled with lust and promises of a better time than she ever imagined.

In fact, he was scaring her a bit, putting her on notice with his intense masculinity.

She shrank back, intimidated by his profound sexuality.

He was coming after her.

It was only a matter of time.

Chapter Twenty

KISS YOU ALL OVER

C onsidering it was Christmas Eve, Holly decided she would tell Luka of Kaine in a couple of days, for sure, after the *Bon Jour* concert. She would have a day or two left after that before Kaine landed.

Kaine!

He was coming, and this happened. Again…

Luka came around from behind the bar shaking out his long, luscious, angel hair. He moved with the grace of a well-bred Englishman. He sat on the edge of her bed, pulling off his snake-skinned boots and then tucked his black socks inside one boot. He neatly placed them at the end of her bed.

Uh-oh.

Luka was in for the night.

Luka Hunter was home.

It started.

"Have mercy," Holly exclaimed quietly under her breath. As his words filled her head.

You're my woman, and I will make love to you, slowly, all night long.

Yes, yes, she knew that!

How long would her allegiance to Kaine survive during another long, loving night with Luka? She expected that by the way she already felt if he touched her for too long, she would instantly surrender.

Panic filled her, tightening its usual ugly grip in her stomach as she realized her tenuous situation.

Silent thoughts slipped in, and she asked.

Which?

Kaine ... Luka?

What do I do now?

No magical intervention occurred. There was only one chance to stop Luka. She would have to face the situation and tell him after he opened her gift. To simply point out that, Kaine was the father of her child and that she loved him against all reason. Kaine deserved a second chance, and as a result, its parents could raise their child.

She predicted that Kaine needed to win this round if she was to go one living with herself and be able to look at herself in the mirror.

Holly leaned over and handed Luka the tiny box making sure not to touch him.

He slid to the floor in front of the Christmas tree and removed the shiny gold Christmas paper as if to savor each moment.

She'd never imagined Luka Hunter to have a tender streak.

He held the box as if it were precious and fragile. He lifted the lid of the jewelry box. Inside laid a solid gold medallion. His initials L.H. were carved on the front. The back carried the simple inscription.

All my love. H

Luka looked up into her eyes. He blew her away. His eyes were rimmed with a thin film of water. He blinked to ward off the tender emotions, banishing them behind his wall of control. But the gentle tone of his voice, edgy and trembling, and choice of words gave him away.

"This is all I've ever wanted from you, Babe. All your love. I have everything in the world, I want. Here put it on me. Please," Luka asked and his face radiant.

She'd forgotten the binding inscription. She didn't want to put it on him. In all the confusion of the holidays and Kaine's nightly gifts, she inadvertently forgotten her sentimental inscription inspired by his continual devotion and Kaine's distance. She'd never meant to infer her love for him at this moment. Especially, in these confusing moments. She felt a strong affection, more like a hot lust for an angel that guided her, keeping her safe while living in the evil valley of her separation from Kaine.

"There for a while, I'd thought I'd lost you." His words cut to her heart.

He did!

Still did!

She'd ordered the medallion before they'd been intimate and long before the arrival of Kaine's gifts of promise for a future. Luka's assumptions were jumping to many wrong conclusions. How could she tell him?

She watched him unbutton his black, silk Asset shirt and pull it open. She sighed. Holly didn't want to look at his golden, suntanned chest that reflected the tiny twinkling Christmas lights. She wanted him to leave before she couldn't ask him to leave. Before she wouldn't. Before it was too late!

"Come on, Babe put it on me. I promise I'll never take it off, never."

Too Late!!!

Reluctantly, she took the gold chain from his palm. But as the pads of her fingertips touched his shoulders, sparks rippled inside her body. She sighed and exhaled.

He sat up on his haunches with his back to her. He moved his shoulders to the sexy beat of the drums pounding from her stereo. His shirt drifted off his shoulders, catching about his elbows, teasing her as if he was an exotic dancer. The season's lights sparkled on his bronzed skin, luring her closer to him. He was seducing her.

He looked up at her, waiting.

Doubts squeezed her conscience as his lust filled eyes called her to him. She felt the blow deep in the pit of her stomach. The noose hung in place, loosely about her neck. If she ran into his arms, she would certainly have enough rope to strangle herself.

Holly held the gold chain in her trembling hands. She watched the muscles twitch in his shoulders as he flinched and threw a long lock of his hair back to settle around his shoulders. The scent of his hair rode on the breeze of his motion. The swift current of air charged at her driving her to close her eyes. Mmmm, the scent of him was intoxicating.

Holly forced her arms to close in a circle around Luka's neck. The medallion hung down in front of him. He was sealed within her personal space. She fumbled, forcing the clasp to close over his thick mane of golden threads.

He shook his arms, allowing his shirt to drop onto the floor in a puddle around him. All he wore was his Levi's. He raised his arms, flexing the muscles of his broad shoulders and pulled his hair up high. It was then she noticed for the first time a small birthmark on his shoulder as she fastened the clasp and hung her flaming desire on him.

It was too late.

Far too late.

Helplessly drawn to him, she ran her hands up his strong arms. She couldn't stop the warmth of him swallowing her. Her hands ran to the end of his, and he interlocked his fingers with hers. The quiet seal of their intimacy banished Kaine from her thoughts.

Luka pulled her down around him into his arms. He cradled her, staring deep into her eyes. His beautiful blue-eyes-to-die for melted into the hot pools of yearning.

Holly's mind and heart were in a race to see which would explode first. Faster and faster, her blood pulsed. She was thankful that she couldn't stop the flow of the intense moments. His feathered hair cascaded down to mix with her sable hair.

He was coming for her.

He enticed her.

Bewitched her.

Pulled her into his masculine magnetism and charm.

His lips parted for a moment.

The rush of lust shot like a bolt of lightning to the top of Holly's thighs. Mmmm, she instantly burned for him. She felt Luka's breath, controlled, yet hot and moist. She watched the pink tip of his tongue dart out to glide across his lips, leaving a glistening sheen. She grabbed a life-saving breath because of what followed. His eyes closed, and he moved closer. His soft lips touched hers, easily, respectfully, and then he pressed more insistently, stirring her as he demanded entrance. His tongue had run along the seam of her mouth before she parted her lips. Her breath ceased. She gasped demanding more. She wanted a full night of kisses. He'd succeeded again. The seduction complete because she wanted Luka Hunter, more than any other moment she'd known him.

This was the time.

Now!

Her feelings were no longer centered in the pit of her stomach. Commitment and confusion abandoned her. She listened to his words of confession meant for his lover, a lover that gave him a symbolic token of her love etched in gold. His sweet, so sweet kisses flooded her face as he opened his heart to her.

"You're mine, Babe. I've loved one woman, but not like you. You're mine, and I want your baby. You're both mine."

And then he kissed her harder, in rhythm to the powerful love song pounding away in the background. It lured her and seduced her. She couldn't think of any way out. She no longer cared. She stretched her arms around Luka's naked shoulders to caress him. She dropped her hand on his muscular back. Her voice betrayed Kaine.

"Luka.., you make me feel ... special ... cherished."

As he continued to ravish her, he took her to the special place where he always did, where no one could find them, somewhere on the other side of oblivion. It was true, she was set on fire by him, and then there were no more thoughts. Only incredible feelings fueled by Luka holding her in his arms, drenched by Christmas lights.

Luka laid her down on his lap as he broke his kiss and raised his head to drop it back. His shoulder length golden strands hair fell back as he gasped for air. His neck stretched, and the corded muscles were covered with a thin veil of perspiration as the sheen reflected the twinkling lights. At that moment, she understood the attraction vampires have for that soft fleshy feast on the side of his neck.

Holly watched the blood course through the large vein pulsating, teasing her.

Luka — aroused.

And if that didn't give him away, then his rock hard erection pressing her lower back did. Yet he kept himself composed, and she didn't understand why.

She was wet for him, so wet it was sinful.

After he'd delighted her with a few deep breaths, making his wonderful chest expand and relax, pressing his flat stomach against the side of her shoulder, he lowered his chin to his chest. And when his eyes locked on hers, she felt a shudder and her breath quicken because he was one fucking gorgeous man.

She reached out to touch his face, her hand trembling. She watched him.

Luka's appetite for her feminine curves flared in his eyes with the curiosity of an experienced lover. His fingers lightly touched her chin and then drifted down her neck over the swells of her breasts, over the top of her stomach and along the side of her thighs. He left a raging firestorm wherever he touched her. She was ready to explode and dared to graze the hem of ecstasy from his provocative kiss, his suggestive stare, and his tantalizing fingers. How would she survive making love with Luka?

He stopped touching her.

She expected he wanted to explore the depth of her. Unfortunately, her floor-length gown stopped him. She was ready for Luka. She reached up and dropped each thin strap from her shoulder to tell him to get the damn thing off her and hurry.

But Luka stopped her.

"No, No. Not yet. First, I bloody well want something to eat. But I promise I'll love you tonight like no other woman in my life. You and I will never forget tonight."

FUCK!!!

His words, powerful.

Holly bit down on her lip and drew blood, excited by his ardent promise. She licked the tainted copper taste of blood away, feeling the intimidation of his promise, knowing he could deliver.

All she could weakly whisper was, "Luka."

The only name on her lips.

"Luka."

But he never changed the name in her heart — Kaine.

This wasn't how it was supposed to be? Yet looking in Luka's lust filled eyes, her hand magnetically ran across his wonderfully broad chest, filled with tight-corded muscles. Not buff, it wasn't as if he found the time to lift a few weights. He was lean, all muscle, and she could easily feel the shape of his bones, and then up his neck. She ran her fingers up the back of

Luka's head, holding locks of his golden strands of hair. She pulled his head down to her, down to where she waited and kissed him with all her feminine charm.

Luka responded quickly. His hard bulge lurched beneath her, and he kissed her long and passionate, unlike any time before, sharing with her a sample of his deep fire for her. He was kissing her like a man completely in love.

How had this happened?

That was the last thought before oblivion blasted into their moment. When he finished with her, Luka rose up before her. His eyes were glazed and sparkling. And there was nothing better in the world than Luka aroused though he left her teetering on the edge of no return.

He'd won, and he stared into her eyes and announced.

"Let's eat!"

"Eat!" She grumbled unable to click off her fiery emotions like a switch.

He grinned accepting the compliment.

"I need to eat, Babe. It's been a while, and I want to concentrate. My personal gift to you — make you scream."

Chapter Twenty-One

WITHOUT YOU

Too late to turn back.

Kaine definitely lost this round to Luka.

Holly never noticed Kaine was erased, banished, and forgotten.

She watched her handsome blonde lover, her man, her boyfriend. No, Luka would never be a boyfriend. He was too much man.

He loomed over her as he stood and flexed his athletic chest. The rippling effect flowed down his smooth stomach. The ravenous sight of him would have brought her to her knees, had she not already been lying on the floor, stretched out with her hand propping up her head. Her long, dark hair cascaded to one side and her full, pregnant breasts, hung seductively to one side. One nipple lay half-exposed while the rest of the long white gown hugged her every curve.

Luka let her know he noticed every inch of her.

"Don't look at me with those ravenous eyes. Pout with those voluptuous lips. Soon, Babe, soon I'll know the depths of you and make all of you mine — forever."

How was a girl supposed to react to that? She lay imagining what he could do to make her scream. Umm, the thought was perfectly delicious.

Luka turned, dressed only in her medallion and Levi's with the top buttons open. The wind of his gait blew his soft hair about his shoulders, moving to a rhythm of its own. His sleek back narrowed to a V and the dark blue Levi's hung maddeningly low on the edge of his slim hips. They were fitted enough to flare her thoughts of his firm round cheeks. His long, lean legs took him to the bar in three strides where he casually threw a leg over a barstool. He sat up straight and regal while he dished out a proper portion of Chinese food. How sophisticated he was spreading his napkin across his lap. If he was anything, he was a gentleman of elegant breeding. And she would bet he would hate to hear that. She stood and watched him serve a smaller helping to her.

"Come on, Babe, eat. Doesn't have to be much. I want all of your attention."

He had that.

She languidly moved and took a step closer, then picked up speed wanting to lose as little time as possible. The current of air that followed sucked the silk, lace robe from her shoulders and she allowed it to float to the floor and rest upon his leather jacket.

She slipped onto the bar stool, real close to him. He reached out with a marshmallow-sized chunk of orange chicken secured by chopsticks and placed the plump morsel next to her lips. She wiped the chicken from the tip with her lips, setting the rhythm she would use later when she loved him with her mouth. She gazed into his sparkling eyes, desperately wanting him.

Luka sat easily in his blue Levi's, his erection temporarily tamed, his attention focused on the scrumptious dinner.

Her eyes drifted to the waistband. The top buttons were freed, and the thought forced her eyes closed. She sighed, lost in a blaring heat. All control of behaving like a lady fled from her thoughts. She was his willing captive once again when the knock came to her door. She was disoriented, wondering how anyone would dare to interrupt these exceptional moments on Christmas Eve.

Suddenly a heavy dose of reality swept over her.

Oh no!

She anticipated exactly what awaited her. Another hard-shelled case meant another note. What would Luka say if he saw the message? Her back muscles tensed.

Luka shrugged off the intruder, his only focus, dinner.

She was embarrassed at how quickly Luka made her forget. And then her usual companion's shame and humiliation scorched her cheeks because she'd realized Luka's intense sexual charisma bewitched her.

She opened the door, hoping to keep the delivery boy out of Luka's view. As expected, the pimple-faced youth stood holding an enormously large box.

"You're back?" She blurted out with surprise, knowing there was no way in hell she could get this large box past Luka, and he'd have questions. She struggled for lies. She struggled for the truth. She tried to think fast for an explanation to explain this parcel. Maybe, he would think it was sent by her parents.

"Yes, Miss Hill," he said as his juvenile eyes popped from

his head, almost as fast as the hard-on in his pants. His eyes were trapped, studying her full breasts.

She looked down and saw they were struggling to be set free from beneath the thin, sheer silk. The cold air blew against her, freezing her nipples to pinpoints.

Fuck! She thought.

His facial expression indicated the same idea.

Holly stood reeling in Kaine's revealing gown. A sexually reactive teenage boy was nothing, realizing how Luka would hit the ceiling when she turned around — too late. She was caught in her web of deceit.

She would have to tell Luka the future held no hope for them.

She waited for Kaine.

Holly generously tipped the kid, stalling, trying to think of a suitable explanation. She quietly took the box and kept her back to Luka. Then, because it was large and bunglesome, the gift took both arms as she casually struggled to walk over and place the huge package under the tree. The oversized gift was wrapped in a bright red wrap, tied with a silver bow, stamped with a large black Asset logo. It dwarfed all of Luka's heartfelt gifts.

Luka filled his mouth like a gentleman. When he'd swallowed, he asked casually.

"When will you open your presents?" Then he cornered a pile of rice, swallowed it, and washed it down with a swig of sparkling apple juice.

"Tradition dictates I open presents Christmas morning." She hoped to stop him and cut off any more inquiries.

Luka returned to his chicken saying, "Come, finish.

You're going to need your strength."

His cool, blue eyes narrowed, telling her he meant now.

As a chill ran through her, it brought a thought she never considered. What would Luka do if she went against him?

As if he'd read her mind, the cool look in his eyes reminded, don't ever consider that.

Kaine once looked at her like that, a long time ago deep down in the black Hell of the corridor. Her head filled with thoughts of Kaine struggling to remind her, to caution her, to get Luka the hell out of her house because he was coming with all his forever love and forgiveness. She was sure Luka felt the change in her attitude.

His cold, blue eyes narrowed once again, and a devilish smile curled about the edges of his lips.

"It's okay, Babe. Kaine won't bother you much longer."

His words stung her. She flicked back a long lock of hair and defensively responded. "Kaine?"

"He's sending you roses?"

As he moved, his arm gestured in a circle around the room. "Hard to miss. The room looks like a bloody hot house for roses."

"Well," she mumbled, stalling. She didn't want to look in his eyes, but she did. Eyes that said he knew the truth, and she'd need not lie to him.

"Yes, Luka, they are from Kaine. He sends them every day." She confirmed, her voice trailing as she sat back on her heels expecting him to explode. To her surprise, his face softened,

After he'd swallowed a long snow pea, he looked down at her.

"I know. It's his trademark. Roses I mean." Luka swallowed a long drink of juice.

"He believes the red roses symbolize his passion. It's bollocks, but over the years has proven effective. Women always fall for them."

Luka's brutal and abusive words crushed her. They sucked every breath from her lungs.

Trademark?

Over the years?

Women always fall for them.

The cruelty of his offensive words burned inside her. She hoped he'd ended his critique. She wanted to throw her hands over her ears, but she didn't, she sat like a prisoner waiting for the executioner to throw the switch.

Luka wiped his mouth and dropped the napkin on his plate. He shoved the plate away from him and twisted on the stool to face her. He closed his eyes, grabbed a quick breath, and then began to explain.

"I found the guitar case and note the first day. That's one of the many reasons I accepted Andrew's invitation, to give you and me time, especially in light of what you told me about London. And I confess, I was angry and ... jealous. Kaine found a way to work his way back into your life. I expected he would at some point. San Francisco was a difficult trip for me. I encounter the usual tarts, in my face. I was ...."

He stopped as if to decide if he would open up to her and tell her how he felt.

"What Luka, what happened?"

"Well, there was this one *lady*, I say guardedly. She was moving quite fast, and I'll confess you before I met you, I'd have happily gone on an adventure with her." He stopped, taking another deep breath and then a chug of juice. He swallowed as if he were thinking about how to tell her.

And suddenly she was feeling hot stabs in her gut at the actual thought of another woman taking her Luka on an adventure! She wanted to scratch the bitch's eyes out! Amazed at her own strong reaction, she quieted herself by saying.

"Are you trying to tell me you slept with her?" Her voice was trembling, knowing his answer, either way, was going to mean something ridiculously important to her. And she didn't like that.

"I'm telling you I didn't. And that was worse. Love is a scary word, Babe. I've been there, I know. I didn't want to feel jealous of Kaine. I didn't want to think of you leaving me — again. I didn't want to feel protective and care about what happens to you and our life together. It would have been easy to forget you and our future in her warm body. But I couldn't Babe. That's when I realized I wanted the entire package, Holly. Fuck! I want all of you. The baby, the family, your love."

Holly sat back dumbfounded.

But Luka wasn't finished.

"Then I realized what a bloody fool I'd been. Nothing else mattered. These past months, it's been you and me building a new world. You've become a big part of my life, Babe. I can't imagine it anymore without you in it. Kaine's fuck up his chance with you, but more importantly — lost it."

Well, this wasn't what she would have expected. She never was able to predict his words or behavior, and it was the same way with Kaine. But his words pricked her, indeed, how could she fool herself into believing Luka would ever give her up without a fight? And this explained Luka's sudden withdrawal and cool attitude at CMT the next morning. What was she doing with this kind and loving man? She was about to tear his world apart over a few dozen flowers and poetic words. Kaine's gifts were supposed to wipe away all the days and hours of Luka's devotion and affection.

Luka got up and walked over to her standing by the tree.

He took her hand. She felt the warmth of his love ooze easily.

"I don't care if Kaine sends you flowers, you deserve them. But what I do bloody well mind is Kaine's inability to accept your mine. Soon he will find out your baby is mine. The three of us will become a family. Perhaps in a few years, we'll have a child of our own. Come on, Babe, don't worry, everything's going to be fine as soon as we tell Kaine. He'll leave you alone when he hears you don't love him and are staying with me, from your lips, with me standing next to you. I'm positive I can make you happy. Haven't I so far?" His eyes searched hers, challenging her to dispute him.

But she couldn't. And she wasn't sure which man she felt sorrier. She didn't deserve either of their attention. But Luka was right. To this point, he'd made her feel deliciously loved, needed, and important. Luka has seen her through a difficult and hard part of her life, and maybe fate brought him here this night of all nights to tell her to forget Kaine. She didn't need Kaine or his legion of demons. And like he read her mind again...

"Face it, Holly. Kaine's no good to you. He's fighting too many ghosts from his past torturing him. I understand you keep thinking about him. That's confusing because you're pregnant, and you feel a strong sense of obligation to Kaine. But let him go, Babe, let him go or...."

"Or?" She quietly challenged. A cold shiver shot up her spine. Luka's tone carried an edge to it, almost hinting a threat. "Or?" she asked again, uneasily, not sure she wanted to meet up with the Luka everyone feared.

"Or I'll put him back in rehab." His words sank like an anchor deep into her soul.

"You knew?"

His face lit up with a charming smile and said matter-of-factly, like shooing away a gnat.

"Of course. Virus! Really? Bloody awful excuse. I would have invented a better piece of hard copy for the press. I wanted to see if you were in contact with Kaine. I knew when you said Emily rang that you were told the truth."

"You were testing me?"

Her internal warning system was ringing loud and clear.

"No, I needed to find out what you bloody well did. And you're good at covering for him, I might add. Kaine would have been impressed with your continued loyalty to the sod. I wasn't angry with you, more amused. But I fancy loyalty in people."

The red-hot heat stung her cheeks.

Loyalty indeed!

"I'm sorry Luka. I was sworn ...."

Cutting her off, dismissing her with a wave of his, hand and he announced.

"I know Babe. I know the drill. I know it all!! I created it!!!!"

Yes, she believed that. How could she have underestimated Luka? She'd never do that again. She pushed her shame aside because her curiosity owned her attention.

"But rehab, how could you predict it?"

"I knew back when he started the cocaine in London. The way Kaine was snorting up large quantities. It was a matter of time. I suggest you forget that lout Kaine, Babe. I'd hate to see something happen to Kaine, something far worse than rehab."

That sounded surprisingly like a threat — again. Was this what Tessa meant when she offered her cryptic warning?

He's capable of murder.

Holly reined in her overactive imagination and gazed at her beautiful Luka. He looked like an angel, and for the first time, she wondered if he was one of Lucifer's angels, as purely evil as he was beautiful. The simple evaluation made her shake her head.

He leaned closer to her and placed his hand under her chin. The soft touch of him washed away the mounting doubts.

No, impossible, she cried out in her mind. Luka could only be an angel with a smudged face. His business dealings would afford him to make difficult choices, but to murder.

Never.

Not this man.

Luka cleared his throat. It would appear he was near the end of the conversation. His eyes swept down her body.

She watched the heat, light up his face, his eyes.

He stared deep into her soul and whispered. "Don't you bloody well worry about anything, I'm here. Put a smile on your beautiful face. Trust me ... Kaine will never have you.

You're mine. You're safe. I'm your manager, your producer and your lover. Soon, I'll be your child's father."

His voice was calm, hypnotic, with a touch of firmness that made her believe him. And her intuition told her it was not in her best interest to dare to disagree.

"And one day soon, your husband. You're mine, Holly Hill. Nothing means anything to me anymore if I can't have you. I'll do anything I have to, to keep you. No one's going to come between us — ever again, or, it will be over my dead body." Luka's face was emotionless like a mask.

She'd no way to understand how far Luka would go to keep her and that thought frightened her. His words, spoken quietly, as if he thought the admission would put her at ease.

It didn't.

Her body quivered as he took her into his arms. He brushed the back of her head with his strong hand. His other arm pulled her close, closer, oh so close to him. She could feel Luka fighting to keep her. She'd underestimated Luka's depth of commitment to her. But, how difficult would it be to free herself from the tangled web he spun around her?

And what about the I.D. bracelet she sent to Kaine? It was to confirm her wishes to start a new future with him.

Did Luka know of it?

He must not.

Somehow, she instinctively understood if he did have that piece of vital information it would be explosive and dangerous for all concerned.

And it was becoming increasingly clear.

If Luka didn't win this round, no one would.

Chapter Twenty-Two

TONIGHT

So far, since Holly had boarded the plane bound for London, none of her plans had worked. Here on this significant and special Christmas Eve, she reasoned, shouldn't be any different.

Luka sat on the floor, and Holly perched at Luka's feet.

She was wondering one thought.

How powerful was Luka Hunter?

And she understood, finally!

Luka Hunter owned her lock, stock, and barrel.

How had it happened?

So much for free will and independence, she supposed she'd exercised. Luka had methodically closed in on her from her career choices to fathering her baby. And she remembered something Kaine said in London.

You'll find what I think means little. Luka runs the show.

How hard Kaine's words hit her this time. She understood firsthand how Luka spun the same strangling web around Kaine for the last decade. Only he didn't have to share his body and make love with him. Luka owned her in a way that

Kaine never needed to fight. Holly looked over at Luka. She wasn't sure if it was with horror or admiration. Especially when she considered the fabulous lifestyle Luka offered her. A successful career, more money than she'd ever dreamed of, reigning status in the exclusive and elite world of music, beautiful homes around the world, the A-list of rock 'n' roll along with international jet-setters as friends. Becoming Mrs. Luka Hunter meant she'd never want for anything.

He'd done the same for Kaine, and she realized the same with Tessa. She was joining an invitation only, private, and exclusive club, where Luka was at the master control. The possibilities with Luka were overwhelming if not mind-boggling. Perhaps Luka was right. He did know what was best for her. Kaine was too late. Kaine remained a momentary distraction because of his surprising gifts and words. It was far too late for them to start again.

Luka would make sure of that.

When her eyes met Luka's, confidence oozed. He'd sealed the deal. His angel face shone brighter than she'd ever seen coupled with a smile that would have dwarfed the sun. He was bewitching her, convincing her to believe him. Too much happened between them. This was not London, but reality, a wonderful reality too good to be true. A reality Luka painstakingly built for her.

He was taking her with him.

Luka stretched out alongside the tree.

Holly was drawn to him, and she crawled up his body placing one hand over the other. Coming close, oh so close, that Luka's orange scented breath drew her to him. His words were soft and sexy.

"This is our night, Babe. Let's not think about decisions, the future, anything, or anyone. It's bloody Christmas. Happy Christmas, my beauty," he reminded his smile was sweet, mesmerizing.

The magic started again, he was casting his spell, and making sure, she would forget.

Holly was trapped in Luka's charming web.

He moved, stood, and helped her to stand next to him. Yes, Luka positioned her right where he wanted her. He was undeniably complex and powerful, and she unexpectedly recognized she liked that.

She was attracted to his power and strength and the fortress that he built to protect her. It was hard to explain. But she always felt safe with Luka, and she predicted he would never allow anyone to hurt her again.

But, who would protect her from Luka if he ever changed his mind about her? That was a thought she dismissed instantly for there was only one. But he wouldn't wait for her forever.

Holly slid her hands up the smooth skin of Luka's abdomen, up to rest on his chest. His legs were apart, and she leaned into the V between his thighs. She then moved her hands up over his shoulders as if drugged and no choice but to bring him sensual pleasure.

And then she couldn't think anymore. He was here, and his hot flesh was making erotic pictures flash in her mind. Quivers began to ripple up and down her body because his cool fingertips were touching her naked back. They were tracing the lines of her muscles and then he rested his full hand on the small of her back and pulled her into him.

Ummm, she could feel the erection filling his pants. It would be soon.

Not soon enough.

Holly leaned and slanted her head to fit her lips fully on his, inhaling his hot breath, the sweet, scented orange begging to be sucked from them. She was so close to him.

"Babe, trust me. I can make any dreams you have come true," he whispered as he turned her over and placed her on the floor beside him and between short kisses. "I promise. I can keep you happy."

Holly responded with barely a whisper, "Luka we're no good together if I can't forget. Come on angel-eyes, make me forget."

Luka needed no further invitation. He pulled the full length of himself up, towering over her and stood. He looked down, and those eyes of his were saying it was time. He held his hand out to her, palm up, waiting.

She placed hers in his, signaling her surrender.

He pulled her up to him. Then his arm swung under her knees, picked her up, and carried her to the cozy bed. He cautiously laid her down, adjusting her body as his weight toppled upon her.

Lost in his lustful eyes-to-die for, she never wanted to be found. To wander about forever in those eyes was her only wish. The ache in her body was thankful it started.

Luka wrapped his fingers around her wrists and stretched her arms tautly above her head. His fingers interlaced with hers as he continued to kiss her madly. It was almost as if to punish her for all the months he'd walked around with this elevated fever of lustful passion. He pressed against her with his hard sex, thrusting into her again and again, with long, maddening serpentine movements.

Holly squirmed beneath him, her sex burning, consumed by a raging fire. Her blood pounded in her head, and between wet, passionate kisses, she cried out for him.

"Luka, please. Don't make me wait. I can't hold on much longer."

"Oh, but you will, Babe. You will wait for me."

"I don't know if I can."

Luka's wet, moist kisses were everywhere. His hot searing tongue licked the inside of her mouth and stroked her tongue. His erratic breath blew on her, a hot wind, fanning her blaze more. He demanded all of her, and she complied. He consumed her, and she was going under, drowning.

Her only fear, she would arrive before he ever undressed her because of too many nights together, too many kisses, too many times touching. The seduction went on for months.

She burned, and there was nothing else he could do but relieve the unbearable pain she felt for him.

"Luka, it's going to happen soon," she cried out again, helplessly lost in his love.

It was as if he knew in each moment, how he deliberately excited her.

He stopped, stared down into her eyes.

Holly didn't know this man, the fireball of lust exploding in his eyes, burning her, wanting her. This was Luka unrestrained, and he scared her. A little. Then again, could it be Luka Hunter was simply too much man for her?

She smiled.

She loved a challenge.

But Luka didn't stop for long. His cool blue eyes studied hers and narrowed, the aloof, sexy smile came back, telling her, he hadn't started.

Fuck! Was the only word impaled in her mind.

Digging in his back pocket, Luka produced a long, black silk scarf. He wrapped it tightly around her eyes. She moved her lips to protest. But she felt Luka's lips crash down on hers swallowing her words between passionate kisses.

He spoke quickly. "Don't. The other night I taught you about how to set your impulses free. Tonight we'll play a game. You do what I say and then use your words to answer."

Holly wanted a breath, to ease the gut-wrenching emotions trapped in her stomach. She tried to tip her head to show Luka she would follow the rules.

Do what he said and use her words.

She could do that, but not, because she was beneath the water of his lust, with no air, lost in Luka's passion.

She was afraid to speak, to tell him she didn't think she'd like that too much. Mostly because she couldn't see his countenance, watch his countless expressions of satisfaction as they crossed his angel face.

She lay quiet, waiting for what he would do next.

She lay in complete darkness and submission.

She felt Luka's hands slide down her arms, he'd been holding over her head until they were parallel to her face. She left her arms stretched above, lying on the pillows. She was breathing in his hot, moist, sweet scent.

He was so close to her.

She marveled at how the blackness heightened the flood of sensations, feeling his breathing so close to her face and then she felt his lips, lightly at first. Then his tongue on her cheek. He drug his tongue along the ridge of her cheek. She didn't know where he was headed. Her mouth opened, hoping to lure him there.

But he didn't.

He stopped.

Because she was flying blind, she couldn't see his eyes and guess what he was planning. Was he simply drinking in the sight of her half-naked, wet, and vulnerable, waiting for her master's touch? Was he thinking about letting the anticipation grow, making her wonder which of a million acts that might please him?

She was afraid if she moved he would stop, afraid if she didn't move he would stop.

Was this a new sample of the tricks Luka learned traveling the world? He was introducing props. How daring making love would be with him.

What had he called it?

Going on an adventure with him.

He finally moved close to her lips, and she was grateful he dropped his hot mouth to cover hers. He pumped fiercely as the length of his body moved on top of her to filled in the peaks and valleys until his hard erection balanced perfectly on her mound. His focused passion thrust into her, rubbing her sensitive rosebud, knowing in a few seconds she would explode.

"Not yet, Babe, wait, not yet. Listen to what I say."

Holly squirmed beneath Luka, and he stopped the wonderful feelings sparking in her from the pressure of him. He stopped his hard erection from pressing her lower belly that demanded, no screamed, to be set free from its entrapment. How long could Luka hold back? How long would these exquisite pleasures continue? And how much more could she endure? She was a simple woman with simple charms. She'd no defense from this world traveler bent on showing her all his expertise.

Impulsively, she jerked, wanting to pull her arms down to a comfortable position.

"No." Luka insisted. "Leave them there. I don't want you to touch me. Not yet."

"No, Luka, please let me touch you since you won't let me see you."

But her pleas were ignored.

He answered with a firm. "No ... not yet."

He kissed her down the side of her neck.

"Do you like this Babe, my lips touching you here?"

And she leaned into him with her head.

"Tell me when I do something you enjoy. I like words while I'm fucking."

His admission shocked her for a moment. But instead of insulting her, in this intimate embrace, fired her. And he felt good touching her. His legs moved to the outside of her body and covered hers, pinning them down tightly. She lay helpless under his weight. She imagined his expression was one of pure delight.

Holly began to speak, slowly at first. "I always want your touch, your fingers, and your hands moving all over me. I want all of your hard ... and soft kisses. I find you pleasing ... no, more than that. I want you hard, especially when you're rubbing against me. I want all of you, Luka."

She pledged naturally, grateful to be with Luka as he thrilled her with his unpredictable tricks.

Luka moved his body to one side of her as his hand slid down the length of her. He lifted the silk gown up her body gathering it around her waist.

Holly felt exposed with the blindfold on laying in the dark. Every sense heightened and on alert. She felt the coolness of the air on her warm skin. His fingertips skimmed across her skin to drop between her legs and then brought them up to penetrate her.

Her body became magnetized, wanting to follow his finger's movements. His magical fingertips pumped her as the sensual electricity flowed from his fingers and her inner muscles wanted to squeeze his hand and make his fingers push her off the edge where he kept her teetering. Suddenly, she understood his plan. He would drive her to madness, and she would never touch him.

Luka moved his lips to kiss her breasts and nipples through the delicate fabric, her neck, and then her mouth. Pulling his fingers from inside her, he moved his hand up and down her body and around her head and pushed them into her hair. He moved his body up against her, then on top of her again, rubbing her with long thrusts, and short thrusts, throwing his leg over her holding her down, then releasing her. He was all over her until she was no longer able to take any more of his unquenchable appetite. From all directions, her passion exploded, with more sounds flowing from her throat than she'd ever imagined possible.

He whispered words in her ear, "You feel great, tell me how I make you feel."

"Wonderful. I'm burning, and it won't stop Luka. Oh...,"

She stammered, breaking her stream of words, her heels digging into the bed, her hands rolling into a ball.

The explosion to bliss too strong.

Surely, she would break.

"...Luka, it burns, deep ..." She heard the contented grunts roll from her throat, no longer embarrassed by the volume of her satisfaction from him.

"Luka ... you're amazing, don't stop. I can feel the need, the burn, do something, Luka."

"I will. This is a good start. You can feel the burn, the longing. It's your turn to show me your love."

She nodded as she continued to explode from the hot rushes.

He kissed her ear and left his lips nesting in her hair. His breath stayed close, moist, and warm, like the liquid that flowed from her body. He untied the scarf and pulled it from her eyes.

All she saw were stars exploding on her eyelids. She lay limp on her back, soaring in the clouds, gliding along the sensual waves that continued at his mercy knowing he'd claimed her complete devotion. A feeling of complete satisfaction crept like a flush across her spent limbs. Well, almost, complete satisfaction.

The thought brought a mischievous smile to her face. He'd proven that he possessed her body and mind. He'd taken them on as easily as the rest of her life.

Luka slid his fingers from Holly's hair, his feet, and legs from around her body releasing her. He slid to the side, his body following the length of hers. He dropped his hand and picked up the leg closest to him, and placed it around his waist, making her legs spread wide apart. He gained full access, and he dropped his hand to probe the deep cavity between her legs, pumping her over the final moments of her flight.

His mouth fell on her lips, swallowing her moans, his succulent lips, and his fiery tongue excited her more. His strong, flexible fingers drew the last of the exhilaration from her. Nothing ever came this close to making her burn like this.

She searched his luscious lips, sucking, and kissing him with a wild, blinding madness.

Luka raised himself up on his elbow, breaking her frantic kiss.

"You can touch me." His hooded eyes said beware, he was about to drop a bomb.

"Tell me that you love me, Babe. Tell me."

She'd little defense, less breath.

She wanted to utter the words.

She was so close, so close, but … but she didn't — couldn't.

"I can make you say it. Babe, I'll do what I have to, but I will do it."

He didn't need to dare her.

Before Holly grabbed another breath, Luka's kisses became more fervent, demanding. He released her leg, placing it beside him and his soft, smooth hand moved up to her shoulders, delicately slipping the straps down one at a time, freeing both swollen breasts.

Luka pulled away. His eyes glowed because he was delighted with her fuller size.

"Your areola is dark, making your nipples look more succulent. Are they more sensitive?"

"Yes," she barely spoke between breaths, then added, "my nipples are ultra-sensitive, and every time you touch them it sends hot, stinging, currents deep inside me. I might explode from your touching them alone."

He smiled. "Thank you. I've never been with an expectant lady. I don't know much. You'll have to teach me."

"Ummm." She murmured, *to teach Luka Hunter*. A perfectly delicious thought.

Luka's fingers curled around the tip of her large, rosy nipple.

Holly held her breath, squirming beneath his deliberate touch, the fire raging inside her. When his mouth touched one nipple, she did explode.

"Like this? ... is this how you like it?"

Her moan was loud as she shoved her nipple back in his mouth. He laid his cheek on her and sucked. Oh, how he sucked, his tongue lapping at the oversensitive bud, the blaze between her legs was overwhelming, following at once on the path of her last climax. "No Luka, I can't don't make me. Not so soon. I haven't any strength. ... Luka."

But she did, and the wave was strong enough to blind her. When her breath returned to a slow pant, he raised his head. He wore a look of surprise and then chuckled.

"This is brilliant. You're responsive to my touch."

"Luka, my whole body is one big fireball. I feel like I will keep exploding over and over, again."

"Precisely my intention. I was concerned full pleasure may take more attention because of your condition. But, on the contrary, we'll learn tonight about how many times I can bring you these loving feelings. This isn't about once Babe, loving is about experiencing the flush and excitement over and over for hours. That's how your body, a woman's body, was made.

"To have one experience is not ecstasy. That's masturbating, getting the sex act over quickly. This night is not about sex, but about loving, trust, intimacy, and the continuing satisfaction after each release, the desires growing stronger than the last, then building to an unimaginable climax. I hope I will take you there."

She'd known that. Another man taught her that! And right now she wasn't about to think of his name.

"I thought you wanted me to wait for you?"

"It's a little late for that. But I'm pleased you feel the burn, the longing and keep coming back for more."

"I will never get enough of you Luka."

"I rather hoped you'd say that. Let's see how much of me you can take?" Luka smiled gently like he understood, but the expression was quickly replaced with his sexy boyish smile that meant to look the fuck out. He dropped his luscious hair all over her chest, as his mouth covered her other nipple, circled, and sucked it to a hard peak. He stopped and looked up at her.

"I love the feel of you. The tint of your nipples has changed again to a deeper color as you peaked. Do you have milk yet?"

"I don't think that comes in until the baby is born."

"Would you share your milk with me?"

His innocent questions inflamed her more, and she tried to

roll up the bottom half of her body because the heat and wetness were too much to take.

He watched her. "Am I hurting you? Tell me if I am."

"Not hurting pain, but a pain yes. Such a pain as I've never known Luka. Hurry, please. I need you to stop it. I need to touch *you*, all of *you* — if you'll let me."

She squeezed her eyes shut before he was able to answer.

She heard his words.

"Touch me, Babe. Show me how I've made you feel."

Then his lips and velvet tongue marked every inch of her swollen breasts. Everywhere he moved tiny fires of excitement were ignited.

Her hand shot down, slipping between the back of his Levi's and his hot skin. She moved as far as she could reach, massaging the warm, lean muscles of his body. She wanted him naked. She wanted to be naked. She was over the thrill of a half-clothed seduction. She hungered for the new challenges of the flesh. She was thinking of a way to free herself from her gown.

Luka repeated. "Touch me Babe." Then returned to kissing her lips while his hands were running up and down tracing her side.

Holly couldn't think. The struggled for a thought to remove his Levi's passed quickly, pulling her hand out of his pants. She ran it up his back and with all her strength, tried to clear her mind and pull him off her. She needed to place him beside her. Finally, when he lay breathing deep breaths, his hair fanned on the pillow and his glittering eyes half opened, she almost swooned from his ravishing beauty. There was nothing more beautiful than Luka fully aroused.

When she could think, she searched for control to ease her breathing. Her hand was instinctively aware of its mission heading toward the next button of his pants.

Damn 501's.

They were difficult to maneuver in the heat of passion. She hurried to drag one button through its hole, then another, then another. Finally, she'd made enough room to reach in and feel him.

Mmmm, he was nothing short of paradise. Hard. Stiff. She wondered if the thin velvety skin would rip being that hard. After many months, many hot and cold moments, she would finally have him and nothing she could think of would stop her.

The gut wrenching sexy feelings returned swiftly, and the wetness between her legs flowed freely. The heat of the moment forced her to demand.

"Take off your Levi's," she stated with such authority, it surprised her.

But he countered.

"No. You do it."

His words were drenched in a huskiness, caught somewhere deep in his throat. His eyes no longer the deep blue she was familiar with, but dark, smoky eyes that were barely opened. They sent her straight to the edge.

"As you wish," she agreed.

Obeying without a moment hesitations, Holly placed kisses down his sensual chest, stopping every few inches to look up to his face.

His eyes are closed.

His hair was spread like a golden liquid across her

flowered sheets.

How perfectly beautiful he was.

Holly planted another kiss and another until she reached his stomach that dipped inward, revealing his huge bulge straining for freedom. Her breath quickened. She followed the trail of dark, golden hair to the edge of his pants. There lay his perfectly shaped pink sex.

She reached in and pulled him free. He sprung to attention a full complement of the man. Long, thick, and strong like him. The golden top glistened from his moisture. A few dark golden curls lay at the base like a soft pillow. The pink color invited her as her eyes feasted on him. She salivated wanting to taste of him, and she was positive she bore that look of starved cat in her eyes.

Holly leaned over and kissed his rising shaft as if paying homage to a powerful sexual deity. All the way down, she planted kisses as she tugged at his Levi's, freeing all of him. Damn, they were hard to maneuver. Holly wanted the Levi's off him, now! She wanted to see all of him, including the luscious plump sack. Her goal was to touch him, kiss him, and make his pink sex ache so he'd have to bury it in her to quench the fire.

She burned for Luka.

The gut-wrenching knots tighten another notch as she kissed every inch of his swelling bulge. She dropped kisses on his soft pouch as she passed on her way to the top of his thighs. She paused, looking up at him and lingered. Her breath quicken again as she rested back on her haunches. Then making sure not to touch his enlarged groin as she struggled with his Levi's, she kissed his knees, the tops of his shins down to the top of his feet.

Holly pulled the cuffs of his pants until his lower body was naked.

At last, the task was complete. What a reward. How unequivocally beautiful and sexy Luka was.

Holly felt great! He'd made her work to free him, and she was hot to have his every inch of him available to her touch, she was about to explode with joy.

"Who do you love, Babe? Show me." He insisted without looking at her. His words surrounded her, coaxing her to move closer.

Holly remembered he would be torturously slow to undress her. She dropped the gown on the floor next to his Levi's.

Holly looked up again, to gaze upon his scrumptious, inviting body. How hungry his body was for her. A slight sheen of perspiration made him appear luminous. His mighty shaft was starting to relax, half-resting, half waiting for her thirsty mouth.

He looked like he belonged in a magazine, not that she'd seen many in her day, but she'd been to college and could state emphatically that he was extraordinary looking.

Holly no longer imagined her future without Luka and accepted the joyous idea of having him fill her bed each night. She would have to forego all daily routines to find the strength and stamina to keep this virile man happy and satisfied.

She delighted in the idea of the challenge.

Was thankful he'd decided to love her.

Happy he'd persisted in the chase and chosen her to love.

He was her every fantasy and so much more.

Luka became many things to her — a controller, gentle lover, fierce animal, passionate man, and arrogant boy. Everything in her body screamed to have him, but she would have to wait.

First, Holly wanted to taste him. To hear his moans caught deep in his chest, trickle up to his throat, to drive him over the edge as he'd sent her. Yes, she would damn well show Luka how he made her feel.

Holly crawled up Luka's body inch-by-inch noticing everything, kissing the hidden freckles beneath the thin covering of hair. His body hair shades darker than his platinum blond streaked hair that grew in thin and sparse. He felt different from her, hard and taunt, he was a man.

Holly was in no hurry, and she would last the night with him if it killed her. She wanted Luka to expect, to anticipate her, and then make him wait, to make him wonder. That was all part of the loving he told her the other night. She was wondering about it, about his large pink sex squirming on his stomach, growing with each inch.

"I see you want me, Babe. Love me. Show me how much you love me. Then I'll show you more."

His words were inspiring.

Show her more.

Holly quickly moved to rescue his sex, kissing his hardened pouch at the base of his shaft, then continued a trail of kisses to the pink flesh, deliberately. She was familiar with how to do this. In fact, her talent, what she did best. She knew she'd gotten to him.

His hands were tangled in her hair. His words short.

"Show me, Holly. Show me."

Holly felt his heels digging into the bed trying to force his strong sex into her mouth. But she'd learned the rules of the game.

Let him wonder.

Let him wait until it hurt bad, and he'd have to be inside her.

Holly laid her head on his abdomen close, so close. Close enough for his musky scent to excite her. Her cheek was burning, branded from his hot, searing skin. She knew he felt her quick breaths on him. Her tongue darted out to lick his mushroomed top, but she wouldn't close in, yet.

His words were quick to lash.

"Holly!" His tone was laced with anguish and desire.

"Holly, suck me! Hard!"

She watched his muscles tighten in his chin, his teeth grinding, his stomach tightened, his legs tightening. Great! He wanted her badly. It would happen soon.

"I want your hot lips to make the fire. Holly, suck, hard."

Good, he was using his words. She'd learned this lesson well.

Luka rewarded her efforts, trying to push her, to guide her head where he wanted, trying to coax her to engulf him.

Holly took her time as Luka taught her, but she teased him more, tasting the drops of his seed as he fought to sustain himself.

"Holly I can't take much more. I've taken too many cold showers in the past few months to last me a lifetime. I'm not a chap that's used to restraining himself. I've done it for you. And only you. There, I've confessed. Please, Holly, do something straightaway before I'm not responsible anymore."

Excellent, she smiled.

Luka was close, but not close enough. His words were sweet and flattering.

Too many cold showers.

This was her area of proficiency. Holly was certain that once Luka got a hold of her, she'd lose any influence she held over him.

She continued taunting, teasing, tasting and kissing him. But she made sure she did not cover him, never took him entirely into her mouth.

"Oh, Holly. You're turning my bloody insides into knots."

Fantastic, he was almost there. She felt his body tense at the waist.

He yanked on her hair hard. She stopped kissing him, to let go with a sharp scream from the pain. He jerked her off his body.

Luka was finished playing.

Smashing! NOW he was ready.

Holly grabbed his hard love and shoved it deep into her mouth. She pulled and milked him with her mouth and her hands.

Luka couldn't hold, but a few moments.

"Holly," he bellowed and froze.

"I'm going to show you how you made me feel," he reassured but with authority.

Holly moved to the edge of his galvanized shaft, ready to plunge down again

But Luka swiftly twisted himself from her and rolled over quickly. He moved too fast, becoming a blur. He pulled her beside him and shoved his hard pink sex into her belly. He let go, lunging and thrusting, the animal in him raging, wild and exciting, wrapping his arms around her body and pulled her to him, pumping with a violence that scared her. His movements were becoming more uncontrollable as he trusted and thrashed against her. Deep guttural sounds slipped one-by-one from his closed throat. His moans were increasing in tone as he grabbed a hold of her buttocks, thrusting one final time, crushing his sex between them and then emptied his hot seed.

Tiny, satisfied sounds continued to cry out from Luka's chest, dying an unmerciful death in his throat. He was trying to control the erupting pleasure she'd brought to him. His body stiffened one last time and then relaxed. His wondrous body broke out in a misty sheen as quickly as the smile spread across her face.

Pleasure filled breaths escaped in waves from Luka.

She took him into her arms and caressed him, ran her fingers lightly over him ending at the base of his spine where she sketched circles on his sweaty back, feeling victorious as his hair follicles stood on end.

She'd done it.

A pleased and satisfying grin sat curled at the edges of her lips. She'd checkmated him. She'd been in control, and she'd brought the longevity required, proving, at least, to herself, she could love Luka his way.

Luka settled on his side, close, his leg wrapped around her. She'd no doubt he was planning her seduction. At least, she hoped.

Holly leaned into Luka and kissed his unblemished chest, kissed the soft dark circle surrounding his nipple. And she felt him move, barely.

He struggled to regain his strength. His gorgeous sexy physique hot and sweaty, the way she loved him. Better yet, she wanted to see him lying stretched out on his back. She wanted to see her fill of him with the Christmas lights reflecting off his ethereal form. To admire and memorize every inch of his fabulously, sexy body, the pantheon of gods gave him to delight her. And wanting him to roll from his side, she nudged him.

Luka obligingly rolled onto his back. His long, silky hair covered parts of his face. His eyes squeezed shut. She watched the heat flush his cheeks, inflaming her. The visual sight of him made her drop kisses on him then sat up on her haunches and did what she wanted to do for too long.

Look at him.

Soak in the radiant beauty of him until her eyes filled to the brim.

He stirred.

She grabbed a quick breath, then panicked and suggested.

"No, don't open your eyes."

"Why?"

She felt embarrassed to say it.

"Tell me, Babe."

In a shy voice, she surrendered. "I want to look at you until I'm filled."

Luka was teaching her about the words. Holly saw the power of her words as his pink sex suddenly lurched threatening to return to life. She grabbed a nearby cloth and brushed back his sun-streaked hair until it covered her floral pillowcase.

She wanted to see his face, the beautiful face of her sexy angel. She treated her hands to a trip across his chest, down his stomach, tracing around his half-resting sex, half-alive. It was as if it never waned. She traced the inside of his thighs and sitting at his feet, she sighed at the wonder of him.

Male, perfect.

Holly took her time watching his chest slow down until his breathing was natural. Holly began to shake her head, and she heard herself say aloud.

"You're fucking beautiful."

He smiled an understanding smile and then pushed.

"What else, tell me?"

No time for words, she was caught in the music pounding out a steady sexual beat, she wanted him inside her, and it was time. It was time to replace Kaine — finally. This would be her conscious choice. She would not be lured, seduced, or driven out-of-control by Luka. With a new sense of herself, she bravely ventured to say in a clear low tone.

"Luka ... open your eyes and look at me. I want you, Luka ... inside me."

There she'd said it.

The moment was fixed with intensity.

Luka said nothing.

But his bright, sparkling eyes expressed it all. He sat up and then scooted to the end of the bed. There, he picked up his Levi's and pulled something out of a pocket. Luka slid along the sheet, bringing her up with him, returning to the head of the bed. He turned and placed a hand full of mints and a few silver foil squares on her nightstand.

He'd been waiting all along for her to ask.

She leaned back. He'd known what tonight would mean — the end of Kaine Walker. Luka arrived ready and prepared to drive her to him. He'd possessed the home advantage and won.

Luka stretched himself out long like a sleek panther, knowing she wanted to see all of him. He urged her in a husky, sexual voice she'd never heard from him, almost a sinister tone, arousing her more.

"Ask me again, Babe.

"Ask me like my woman.

"Convince me, you're my woman."

Fuck!

Holly didn't understand why words during sex, were more arousing than she'd imagined. The idea to ask him to have sex was different. She'd realized that she'd assumed he would go ahead as most males. But then in his line of work, he was used to women asking him to have sex. She looked into his eyes, and they glowed unnaturally, seemingly unearthly, perhaps with a hint of contradiction.

She was mesmerized.

She didn't want to betray him, deceive him, or lead him on to believe a lie. To hear the flesh and blood of Luka speak at a time like this was impressive. He was human like anyone else and needed to be loved, told he was loved for himself, that he alone was enough for her. And he was much more than enough.

Holly bent to show him, to kiss his thighs and hurried up to his hard sex.

"I don't hear you, Babe."

She was moving closer to him. She kissed the tip of him

quickly, tasting the last of his seed, as she placed her lips on him firmly, covering him, and sucked. He'd taught her he liked the sounds of sex as she methodically sucked on him, noisily and impetuously.

Luka responded by producing an astonishingly stiffer cock.

Holly hadn't been sucking long when she felt him pull hard on her hair. Again, her mouth released him, forcing a yelp from her.

Luka changed.

He was raging, demanding.

"You want me? Here." He roughly tossed her a condom.

She hurriedly ripped it open, pinched the top, forgetting she'd learned the trick from Kaine. She rolled the thin sheath down his large, steel sex in a panic, fearing it wouldn't fit, then positive the size of him wouldn't fit inside her. She required no preparation. Her sex was wet and ready. She moved with the quickness of a hungry cat and with the finesse of quicksilver to lie beneath him.

However, Luka's great strength pulled her out. He entertained other ideas, and he pulled her up to a sitting position on top of him. He swiftly separated her legs wide, to bend on his sides.

She wrapped her hands around his neck. She looked down in his sexually, hot blue eyes. She blinked, giving him the signal to go.

But Luka didn't move.

Oh no, now what?

"Talk to me. Ask me, Babe."

"What do you want from me, Luka?"

She couldn't think.

She'd give him whatever he wanted.

Say anything he wanted.

Tell her.

She felt the full length of him putting the flames out inside her that raged like a monsoon attacking a firestorm. She dropped her forehead to his shoulder.

"Tell me what you want me to say? I'll say it. Please."

"Start with telling me you're mine. Tell me you love me."

"Oh, Luka, you know I do. Since the first moment, I saw you. I've always wanted to be your woman. I am your woman damn it! Take me before I explode without you."

But it was too late.

Her own confession excited her. She felt the white-hot rush like the sound of a tornado blowing through her starting at her toes.

Luka showed no gentleness, no tenderness, raw, male, sexual magnetism as he pushed his way inside her.

As she began to release, the pleasure turned out to be too great. Hot tears sprang from her eyes.

He was inside pumping her, hard and fast, hard and faster, the burning heat rippled through her like fire burning lace. It washed over her again and again, as she wiggled her lower body to accommodate his enormous size.

He groaned deeply.

"Ummm, you're fucking tight Holly." She heard him say as her release rushed again. Hot sizzling sensations sprayed like shrapnel everywhere, splintering her body. Her head sprung back as if blown off her body. And her back arched as she slid to the base of him. Her loud, animal groans were the only sounds to fill the cozy room.

Luka's powerful hands held her at the base of him grinding into her deeper and deeper, and the moans of penetration escaped from his throat. His voice was low, filled with sensuality.

"You feel like I need to fuck you for a long, long while."

Again, the waves of ecstasy flooded her. Would these sensations ever stop? Would each thrust of Luka bring another release and another, and another until she was paralyzed with ecstasy? Would she simply die from the intense bliss of Luka Hunter?

He drove his hot sex of a molten blade deep and deeper inside her.

His demons compelled him too, and his strong hand held her lower back, shoving him deeper. He moved, shoving himself in, lifting her, withdrawing an inch, and in again, harder and faster. In and out, deeper each time until he reached the top of her. And his promise came true as he hit the top of her, forcing the screams, screams of excitement loudly filling her room.

The animal in both of them exploded.

"Again, Luka, do it again. You feel so fucking good."

And he did.

"Again, and again," she repeated. "Harder, faster, harder, again," she yelled out until her fluid ran thick and smooth, allowing Luka to move about freely inside her.

"Luka, again," she declared with excitement.

"Show me, Holly. Show me how much you love me. Love me hard, let it go. I can take it."

And she did.

She erupted with new, deeper feelings and she let loose, feeling sensations she'd never experienced before Luka. She wanted to collapse on his chest, but his hand covered her derriere, sending more deep quakes and quivers throughout her already sexually drenched body.

Luka moved in and around, faster and faster, pushing himself to her summit and she heard her screams. He would slow down as if to let her rest. Then the maddening rhythm began again taking her to another feverish peak. And he would not let her go. And again he slowed and began the build up again. She was going crazy with ecstasy, her body lost to his commands. She opened her eyes and saw his eyes were shut, his face strained, his muscles taut and his flesh hot, pink and glistening from the sweat. She heard her own cries again and again.

"You're hot, wet, from me. I'm bringing the fire and only I can quench it. Tell me, who brings the fire?" He challenged in her ear.

"You, only you." She whimpered.

After a while, she was weak from pumping him, weak from her trip to shimmering bliss, weak from Luka. He was strong and nothing she offered tired him. She tried to lie down on his chest, but he pushed her back up taking all of him. Her back arched, making her scream while his hands fondled her breasts. Each time his thumb caressed her sensitive nipples, lightning fired inside her. He held her up, and her sex-drenched, hooded-eyes drifted to his. He held her gaze transfixed. Luka showed her every emotion hiding inside him.

She blinked.

She couldn't believe what she saw.

She must be delirious.

Staring deep into his unguarded blue eyes, she saw it — she saw the evil.

Did she do it again? Make a fool of herself?

No one controlled Luka Hunter, in or out of the bedroom. He'd let himself climax. Luka could have stopped. But he'd gotten it out of the way, his intent, to fuck her to death. He'd done it again. He'd lured her into his web, and she was helplessly tangled in it. And the more she struggled, the more he made her scream.

The pleasure became too painful. If this was war, his plan worked. She shuddered, suddenly afraid.

Luka was the one in control — always been, always would. That was the message. He'd done this with her from the starting, proving she was in way over her head. What would Luka Hunter do with her? For the moment, he would fuck her long and hard until he was finished. And if he were true to his word, this would take him all night long. She looked down, barely able to speak from the joyous sensations filling her body. Pleading with his hard, cold blue eyes, seeing his lips move, the words he spoke frighten her.

"Ask me, Babe."

Perhaps if she asked nicely, he would let her lay down on his body.

"Please, Luka please."

It worked. He let her lay down on his chest. She cooed like a baby as she laid her head in the crook of his neck. His strong protective arms embraced her, cradling her as if a child. One thing was loud and clear, she was no child, and she *was* Luka Hunter's woman. She belonged to him, and she didn't want to be around if anyone disagreed.

Luka's hand went to her chin and with a bent finger. He tilted her chin up, allowing him to drink from her lips. His kiss was like an oasis in the dry desert of her mouth. His kiss magical in her parched mouth, wet and moist giving her life. And he never stopped, no, never slowed his steady pumping inside her. His never tiring sex pounding, running chills up her back, and hot excitement down her body.

She flowed wet and hot for him.

Never enough... never get enough.

She knew then she would never resist him. She was out of tricks. She'd surrender to whatever he wanted. And if how he made her feel was how Luka Hunter's woman should feel, then yes, she was Luka's woman, totally his.

Holly felt Luka relax his body, a little. She lay in his arms, and she couldn't stop him from loving her. She was right about one thing, he felt fantastic inside her. Natural, tight, but a bit too long to take all of him. She nestled her head along the column of his neck to rest, sweat beads on his neck clung to her. At the same time, she spread her legs further apart, taking in more of him and then wrapped them around his lean legs. Her hand slid up to rest on his cheek.

Luka moved, turned her over to her side, and then laid her on her back, following her to lie on top. His silky golden hair fell into hers, and his gorgeous blue eyes stared straight into her soul.

Her half-hooded eyes watched him, watch her. And she threw back her hair to let him see the waves of his decadence lashing her body.

He rose up, his lower back, thrusting his sex inside of her

with long thrusting motions making her wetter if possible.

"Tell me, Babe, tell me," he demanded.

She knew what he wanted to hear. But could she say the words aloud? Her body already told him loud and clear. Her sexual appetite heightened instead of diminished. Her body followed his. He was strong, so strong, never stopping. Powerful, he filled her with a mixture of a million thrilling sensations.

She heard the words tumble, quietly at first. The words declaring the commitment he was determined to hear. Both knowing as she spoke them aloud, she would never go back to Kaine.

And then she understood that was his intent — to fuck Kaine Walker out of her.

"I ... love you ... I do love you ... Luka."

"Louder!"

"I love you."

"Louder!"

He thrust his strong, fiery sex as high inside her as possible and then froze.

"Louder!"

She screamed the vow all the way to England, exactly as he intended.

"I love you, Luka ...."

TO BE CONTINUED...

She can have anything she's ever wanted…

Holly Hill is traveling in the American Southwest with the sexy Luka Hunter, her manager, and producer, living the fast lane lifestyle. Luka has promised her the 'sky is not the limit.'

Except what she wants…

However, her tender heart cries out to love the brooding rock star Kaine Walker. Her sweet memories of him torment her because she carries an unbreakable love and bond so strong it supersede her duplicitous deception with the attentive and romantic Luka. She is hiding a deadly secret from Luka that puts her in constant danger and keeps her trapped behind her confession to loving him.

Is his commitment love…
Or obsession?

http://www.kewtownsend.com/

KEW TOWNSEND

Forthcoming:

Affairs of the Heart ~ Hollywood
BLOOD (Part 1), *LIASION* (Part 3), *DECEPTION* (Part 4)

Affairs of the Heart Series ~ London
HEART (Part 1), *TEMPTATION* (Part 2)
PROMISES (Part 3), *DEVOTED* (Part 4), *BETRAYAL* (Part 5)

Ms. Townsend is a widow with a wonderful daughter, educator of school-age students, travel and movie buff, and writes romantic music fiction set in the 1960s-1980s rock scene in the *Affairs of the Heart Series*. She lives in sunny Southern California and loves to read under a palm tree with wave's crashing along the shoreline.

KEW's love of rock music began at a young age when she returned glass Coke bottles for change to buy 45 rpm records. Her interest moved from the music to the musicians, and living in Hollywood, interviewed the Beatles when they landed at Los Angeles International Airport. Acquiring a taste for the funny Englishmen, she began dating one of the Rolling Stones that exposed her to sex, drugs, and rock and roll. Later her memories surfaced in the *Affairs of the Heart Series* where she weaves her behind the scenes anecdotes with her long love of castles, mysteries, lightning, and thunder into a romantic suspense story. Her master's degree in Cultural Anthropology and Archaeology adds to her world travels, and flavor to her novels.

CONTACT KEW

kewtownsend.com

Leave a message, a review, and sign up for the NEWSLETTER. Be first to hear about new releases, preorders, sales, prizes, giveaways, and fun events.

www.ingramcontent.com/pod-product-compliance
Lightning Source LLC
Chambersburg PA
CBHW050037180626
46810CB00002B/775